# The Book of Color

# The Book of Color

A NOVEL

~ Julia Blackburn

PANTHEON BOOKS   NEW YORK

Library of Congress Cataloging-in-Publication Data

Blackburn, Julia.
The book of color : a novel / Julia Blackburn.
p.   cm.
ISBN 0-679-43983-8
I. Title.
PR6052.L3413B66    1995
823'.914—dc20    95-6620

*Book design by M. Kristen Bearse*

Manufactured in the United States of America

First American Edition

9  8  7  6  5  4  3  2  1

*for Hein*
*and our children,*
*Natasha and Martin Thomas*

# Acknowledgements

In Mauritius I am especially grateful to Philippe and Jeanne Blackburn, Sanjeer and Sunita Djaiboo, Evalina Larose, and Bernard and France-Marie Perrine. I would also like to thank Jane Alexander, Joan Blackburn, Tanya Bocking, Judy and Phyllis Downie, Toby and Isobel Eady, Dan Frank, Dan Franklin, Richard and Julie Hamburger, Liz Loftus, Susan Paine, Basil Saunders, Michael Schmidt, Tim and Patsy Swann, Bruce Wallace and Janet White.

When I came back from death
it was morning
the back door was open
and one of the buttons of my shirt had
disappeared.

DERICK THOMSON,
*Return from Death*

# Part I

# One

It was once thought that when your house had been visited by the plague, then it was a good idea to shut a pig in the infected rooms and leave it there for a day and a night. In the morning you could open the door and drive the pig into the world and it would take the sickness with it when it went, so that you and your family could return home in safety and all would be well.

I look at the pig: pink and tight-skinned and as naked as only pigs and people can be. I look at the house which has frightened me for so long. I open the door and the pig goes racing into the hall and up the stairs; I can hear the hammering of its sharp feet on the floorboards; I can hear it squealing as it moves from room to room and I can easily imagine the mad gleam in its pale eyes.

When morning comes I open the door and the pig rushes out and disappears.

# Two

O r perhaps there is nothing to stop me from going into the house with the pig; the two of us standing together outside the front door while we wait in uncertainty, the pig leaning its heavy body against my leg so that I can feel the warmth of its life. If I keep very still then maybe I could feel the pattering of its heartbeat and hear the rhythmic sound of its breathing, like distant waves breaking against a shingle beach.

Everything is very quiet, hushed; even the bird singing in a tree close by seems only to emphasise the silence. It's not that I am sad, but I am solemn with all the solemnity of childhood. I have come back to a place I once knew and I am uncertain about what will happen next. I am also afraid, but I must not forget that I have the pig to keep me company and the pig has nothing to be afraid of.

Suddenly the door swings open and there is my

grandfather. I haven't seen him for a long time but I recognise him immediately. His thin white hair floats like a morning mist above the shining dome of his skull, his skin is waxy yellow, his eyes are almost black, his bottom lip quivers. When I was a child I was mesmerised by the quivering of that lip.

My grandfather smells of camphor and peppermint and something rather musty. Camphor to protect the clothes from moths that might otherwise set up residence within the fabric, peppermint to clean the breath and something rather musty to be hidden in boxes and cupboards and even in pockets where it rustles about and tries to find a means of escape. Without a word he takes one of my hands in both of his and I look at the scrubbed fingernails. His hands are curiously cold, soft and reptilian. The pig grunts thoughtfully close to his polished shoes, but he does not appear to have noticed it. He lets go of my hand and turns to lead the way into the library which is dark even though the day is bright outside. The pig goes to sit under the mahogany table while I stand in the middle of the room and watch my grandfather as he sighs and mutters to himself before settling into an armchair and staring comfortably into vacancy.

A coal fire is burning in the grate and on the mantelpiece above the fireplace there is a bronze statue of a naked Greek youth who is perched on a tree stump and preoccupied with the task of pulling a thorn out from the sole of his foot. As a child I was fascinated by this dark nakedness that glittered in the firelight. When no one was looking I used to run my fingers along the rippling length of the bronze vertebrae, stroke the thighs, touch the metallic curls on the head.

To the left of the fireplace there is a portrait of Jesus as The Light of the World. He is standing in a dark garden and holding up a lamp which shines under his chin, making him appear very menacing, especially around the eyes. To the right of the fireplace there is one of my grandmother's water-colours. Most of her paintings are of orchards with blossoming trees or soft hills receding into a far distance, but this one shows a sunset over a calm sea and it looks as though quantities of blood have been poured into the water during a fight between two monsters of the deep. A great thrashing and tearing of flesh followed by stillness.

I wonder where my father is. I have the sense that he must be somewhere close by, but I haven't seen him yet. I imagine him wandering through the garden, lumbering forward step by step while the heart pumps the alcohol, the thoughts and the drugs round and round through the arteries and along the delicate tracery of the veins. Largactil and Parstelin and all the other wonderfully named chemical compounds mix together with Long Life beer and Jamaican rum, with a

passage from *The Tibetan Book of the Dead* and the opening
lines of a new poem that he has just written in a shaking hand over and over again in a little red notebook.
He pushes his way past the tangle of rhododendron
bushes and ducks his head too late to avoid the overhanging branch of the cedar tree. He staggers but does
not fall. He coughs and stares and grinds his back teeth
together so that you can see the muscles of the jaw
flickering across the cheeks. He could look terrifying
and I often used to think that he was on the edge of
turning into something that was no longer human; a
werewolf perhaps, or something like a werewolf. I
remember him growling under a table, I remember
him screaming in the darkness, but for the moment I
am in the house in which he grew up and for the
moment it's as if I have become him as a child, stepping
into his skin and staring around me with his eyes. I
wonder if that makes sense. Is it possible to inherit
memories just as well as the colour of eyes and hair, the
shape of lip or nostril? Is it possible that I can seem to
remember my father's childhood as if it was something
I had experienced myself, and could this process be
allowed to move back through the generations as far as
a person wished to take it? Could I choose to remember
my grandfather's childhood even though he never told
me anything about it; perhaps never told anyone once
he had left it behind?

I stand in this dark room and look at the french windows that glint into the garden. I look at the glass-fronted bookcase filled with leather-bound books so tightly packed together they could be carved out of a single lump of wood. I look at the gold and enamel clock standing on curled dragon's feet within its glass dome and I watch the swing of the pendulum that is shaped like the sun with a smiling face on it. I look at my grandfather sitting in his armchair as distant and impassive as a tortoise and all at once I can see him as a young man, with his hair black and shining, his teeth white, his lip no longer trembling. He is chasing the child who was my father round and round the table beside which I am standing. He is chasing that child and lashing out at him with a leather belt, the metal buckle gleaming as it swishes through the air in search of its quarry. The child is screaming and I can feel the sound thickening around him as if trying to protect him from harm.

Much later during that same evening and many other evenings as well, the old man my grandfather in his good-looking youth can be seen going up the carpeted stairs to where my father as a boy is sleeping. In his hands he is carrying a glass bowl half filled with a mixture of peroxide and the juice of a lemon. He opens the door and goes into the room with its lines of regimented roses on the wallpaper and a little latticed window framed by the ivy that grows up the wall on the west side of the house. He kneels quietly beside the bed where the boy is sleeping and slowly, perhaps even tenderly, he begins to wash the child's face with a wad of cotton-wool dipped into the liquid.

The child wakes up abruptly, the bleach stinging his skin, catching like a sharp hook at the back of his throat. His father says, 'You have been out in the sun, that is why your skin is too dark. Keep still, this will help to make it better', and he continues with his work, careful to avoid the wide staring eyes.

Nights become days, days become nights, all this is long ago. Here where I am now it's almost four o'clock and the air is thin and cold. When I look out of the window I can see the silhouette of a wren sitting on the silhouette of a tree. The sound from such a tiny bird is so loud and strident it seems to have the strength to cut through all these other thoughts, pulling me back into the present. There are only two apples left on the apple tree, the rest have fallen or have been picked. I try to imagine the frogs that must be sleeping in the mud of the little pond, as still as stones, breathing through their reptilian skins.

# Three

In spite of the bird that is still singing as if its life depended on the song, I find that I am once again back in that darkened room with the pig and my grandfather for company. The world outside the long windows looks curiously white and flat; maybe it has been snowing or a mist has come in from the river. I hear the sound of footsteps on the stairs, voices. My grandfather has taken a peppermint out of his pocket and after the complexity of removing it from the wrapper, he is sucking it noisily. The pig is making wet snuffling noises under the table. I think it must have found something to eat.

Once when I was a young child I was standing here in this room when the door opened abruptly, letting in a tiny frail man I had never seen before. He can't have been much taller than I was and his body was bent over as if he had been carrying something that was far too heavy for him. He was wearing a grey suit, his hair was grey and as I see him now even his skin had a greyness to it. He was holding something in both hands; I think it was a book but I am not quite sure. His whole body was trembling in the way that leaves can tremble on a tree, but I had never imagined that anything like this could happen to a person. Every part of him seemed to be flooded by a useless rush of electricity. He went to stand close to my grandfather and said something to him very softly and even though I could not distinguish any of the words I could tell that his voice trembled as much as his body did. He placed the object on a side table close to the fireplace and then he left the room.

'Poor man,' said my grandfather when the shaking man had gone and I was shocked to realise that he was talking to me because usually he never spoke to me once the formality of a greeting had been completed. 'Poor man. He fought in The Last War. He was in the deserts of North Africa and he was buried in the sand by black men. They buried their enemies up to the neck in sand and he was lucky they did not cut away his eyelids; they did that sometimes and your eyes were burnt out of their sockets by the rays of the sun. Then the black men would gallop with their horses over the heads of the men they had buried. Think of that.'

And I did. I thought about it a great deal, especially at night. The rows of heads like cabbages in a bare field and the anxious expression on all their faces as they listened for the approach of the horses. The little man who was no taller than me, preparing to die in an enormous desert, held fast by the yellow sand that gripped his arms, his legs, his frail body. I presumed that he must have been buried slightly apart from his friends and that when the hooves thundered over their heads, breaking them like crockery, he was left unscathed. I wondered if he saw what was happening or if he closed his eyes until everything was quiet again. I wondered if the black men realised how frightening this all was. For some reason I pictured an aeroplane flying in the blue sky, the sun glinting on the metal and the pilot looking down and seeing a solitary head in the sand. So the plane circles and lands and the pilot digs the man out of his captivity, but he starts to shake as soon as he is set free.

It can't have been long after he told me this story that my grandfather contracted Parkinson's disease which meant that he was soon shaking as well. He was unable to hold a cup or a spoon and sometimes when he was making his slow progress from one side of the room to the other, he would have to wait while the tremors rattled through his body like a fierce wind, a hurricane.

And then my father began to shake. His hands, his face, his whole body that had grown so heavy and cumbersome, trembling as delicately as an aspen leaf. I suppose that was why the idea of the man buried in the desert fixed itself so vividly in my mind. It seemed to contain a clue that would explain something if only I knew how to begin. And the more I thought about it the more it seemed as if it was me who had been there, staring out at a vast landscape and listening for the approach of horses ridden by wild men with black faces.

# Four

The pig knocks its heavy body against the
carved leg of the table, causing a glass bowl to
perform a brief dance on the polished surface of the
wood. I see now that it is eating a book; one of those
leather-bound volumes that had seemed so solid and
immovable. It has managed to tear off part of the cover
and its strong jaws are in the process of turning the old
leather into a brown pulp. I suppose it could be pigskin.
I wonder how the book came to be on the floor in the
first place. I wonder if the pig will be interested in eating the thin pages as well. My father once told me that
a pig would eat dead cats and cinders, something which
I thought was such an odd combination. He also told
me of a murderer who cut up his victim into little
pieces which he fed to his pig, but the pig spat out the
teeth and that was how the crime was discovered. It is
extraordinary how all these stories came to life with
the telling of them: the pig standing there with its head

down, the ears blinkering the eyes, the tail curled and twitching and the unwanted teeth heaped up in a little pile on the concrete floor of the sty.

There is a scuffling noise outside the door. The handle turns and the pig looks up expectantly, a scrap of leather protruding from the corner of its mouth.

My father enters carrying a briefcase. His head is tilted sideways as if the ceiling was too low for him to stand upright. His shoulders are hunched, his arms hang loose. He smiles as he gazes around the room but I am not sure if he sees anything at all. He goes over to the bookcase, examines the line of books behind the glass doors and seems to be searching for something in particular. He rattles impatiently at the little brass handles and when he cannot get them to open he punches with his clenched fist into the thin glass. He cuts his hand and sucks the blood that drips from the wound. 'All the perfumes of Arabia will not sweeten this little hand,' he says thoughtfully, wiping his fingers on his white trousers so that they leave a smeared trail on the cloth.

It is only then that he notices the old man his father who is sitting hunched and unperturbed in a chair by the fire. He walks towards him, with a curious mincing step, and he is still carrying the briefcase with his arms extended stiffly like the wings of a penguin. He pulls up another chair by the fire, opens the briefcase and takes out a battered packet of cigarettes. I look at his hands which are red and swollen as if they have been left out in the cold and are suffering from the first symptoms of frostbite, but at least the bleeding has stopped. The hands tremble as he tries to grab hold of a cigarette and when he has got one he brings it with infinite slowness to his lips before reaching into his pocket for the matches.

The first match snaps in two as he strikes it. He manages to light the next one, but holds it head down so that the flame engulfs his finger and I can smell the acrid burning of the nail. 'Ouch!' he says, and drops it to the carpet where it smoulders and dies. With the third match the cigarette is finally brought to life and my father puffs heavy mouthfuls of smoke into the air, while my grandfather watches him and sucks at a peppermint.

I feel lonely. I crawl under the table and sit next to the pig. The two of us stare out from the safety of our shelter like early hunters in their cave. We must be quick to decide when we need to run and when we need to give chase.

My grandmother comes into the room carrying a tray of tea and biscuits. She is wearing a long skirt that makes a swishing sound as she walks. Her face is masked by a layer of white powder and an auburn-coloured wig sits comfortably on her head like a sleeping cat. She sets the tray down on the little table close to the fireplace and then withdraws. As she walks past me I am tempted to pull at the hem of her skirt. It's not that I want to startle her, it's just that I long to break the spell in this room, the oppression of silence. But I don't move and in the next moment she has gone.

Neither of the two men makes any attempt to drink the tea which waits for them in cups of thin bone china, but my father stretches out his hand for the biscuits. He takes them all and drops them into the pocket of his jacket, then he stubs out his cigarette on the empty plate and clears his throat with that odd ringing sound that I used to hear so often echoing through the houses of my childhood. It was like the cry of some night animal prowling through the forest; a strange sound that was both fearful and filled with fear.

'Must go', and he rises to his feet so abruptly that the chair falls over with a clatter. He places both hands on his father's shoulders and bends forward to kiss the grey stubble of his father's cheek. In spite of the difference in age they do look very similar; it's not only that they share the same foreign darkness of skin and eye but they have the same haunted expression as if they were both hemmed in by identical ghosts.

# Five

I look at the pig. The pig steadies me. It has finished with the book and is pushing its nose expectantly among the woven flowers of the carpet. Biscuit crumbs perhaps; mud from boots; dust from all the things that turn to dust eventually. Nothing substantial for a pig to eat but enough to keep it busy for a while.

I sit very close and it watches me with pale eyes that are almost without colour, like frozen water or a winter sky. I sit close, careful not to disturb it with any sudden movement. I run my hand gently along the length of the stiff back: the heat of the skin, the roughness of the bristles. I scratch the shoulder where the front leg joins with the solid flesh of the body. I watch as the pig's eyes begin to flicker and close, it sways on its feet and then slowly, slowly, it collapses to the floor, lying there in a trance, the thin legs stretched out, the mouth gaping. It reminds me of a bullfight I was once taken to when the bull knelt with a bowed head in front of the matador who was killing it and then rolled on its side into the trampled dust of the bullring with such an easy grace. But the pig is not dead, it can jolt back to life in an instant.

My father and grandfather are still there by the fireplace, the one bent forward to kiss the cheek of the other. And now I see that they are starting to move. My father puts an arm around my grandfather's waist and lifts him to his feet. They stand together entwined like lovers and they begin to dance. Round and round they spin in this darkened room: one two three, one two three, one two three, avoiding the furniture as they go.

I crouch under the table with the pig, observing the dancers. Sometimes their big feet tread close to where I am concealed and then I must be careful because they could easily step unnoticing on my fingers.

My father is wearing his favourite white linen suit which has become much too tight for him so that it looks as though he has been poured into it. His knees are bent, his chin is to his chest and he is grinning like a crocodile. I doubt if he would see me even if I came out from under the table and grabbed hold of his arm. He is turning faster and faster with the old man my grandfather clasped within his embrace and almost hidden from view; just the white glint of the dog-collar, the white mist of hair.

The clock within its glass dome begins to strike the hour: hing dong, hing dong, hing dong dong dong. With a squeal of surprise the pig jumps to its feet and races towards the open door, knocking against the legs of the dancing men as it goes so that they stumble and must surely fall to the ground. I do not wait to see what will happen next. I follow the pig out into the hall, up the stairs, along the corridors.

I follow the pinkness of the pig. I follow the hammering of its feet and the shrill screech of its voice. We pass endless rooms and each room is filled with something that is happening: all the years of my childhood stuffed into rooms where people scream and cry, struggle together and fall apart. I see my father crouched on all fours barking like a dog with his teeth bared; I see him lifting a chair and smashing it through a window so that the shattered glass falls like snow; I see him collapsing to the ground in the heap of his own body and lying there, sobbing like a child. But I follow the pig.

# $S$ix

We run and run and then we stop running and walk quietly side by side into a room that I have never seen before. Everything about it is unfamiliar; the walls are made from the rounded trunks of trees, the floor is a rough pale wood. There are two big windows with white curtains billowing in the wind and these windows have no glass in them. The air is very warm and sweet smelling. I can hear the sound of the sea breathing in and out. I can hear the electric rippling song of a strange bird, a woman laughing, a dog barking.

My grandfather is sitting cross-legged on the floor in the far corner of the room. He looks older and smaller than he did before and very dark-skinned in this bright light, but the shaking seems to have stopped. He licks his lips with a pink tongue and yawns. He has a wooden box on the floor beside him and he has taken out all the things it contained and set them

in front of him like the pieces in some mysterious
board game. There is:
  – a snail shell
  – a silver crucifix on a chain
  – a long white feather
  – a branch of red coral
  – a battered tin box such as might be used to contain pills
  – a crab's claw
  – a shining black nut, larger than a human head,
the skin like human skin black and glistening, the
shape like the hips, the thighs and the triangular sex
of a woman. Obviously this was too big to fit in the
wooden box. He must keep it somewhere else.

'Ask him,' says the pig and I am not at all surprised
to hear it speak. 'Ask him what these things are and
why he has kept them. Ask him to tell you where we
are and then he might begin to remember some of his
life for you.'

'Where are we, Grandfather?' I say. He looks up at
me and I can see my own face reflected in his dark eyes.
He is silent at first and I am afraid that he can't hear me
or that he has lost the power of speech, but finally he
does answer in a strangely monotoned voice as if he
was talking in his sleep.

'Where are we? We are on the island of Praslin, one
of the little Seychelles islands in the Indian Ocean and

seven hundred miles north of Mauritius where the poor dodo died.'

'But what are we doing here?' I ask him. 'Why have we come?'

'Why? Because I was born here, 1880. Funny place to be born since no one has heard of it. But General Gordon who was killed in the Siege of Khartoum came here in 1881 and he said that this was Paradise. He said that before the great ice caps of the north melted and caused The Flood, there was a land called Lemuria stretching all the way from Madagascar to India and everything was swept under the water except for Paradise which was on a high mountain. And that's where we are now. The General worked it out on his maps.'

'And did the General come here?' I ask.

'Oh yes, on his way to India or on his way back from India, I'm no longer sure. But he wanted to see if he could find the Tree of Knowledge of Good and Evil and he found the coco-de-mer, the sea coconut, and was sure that was it. There is a whole forest of them growing in the centre of the island in the Valley of May and the General said he had never been to a place that was so lovely, so cut off from the rest of the world. The trees grow to a height of over a hundred feet and the males and females stand together in pairs. The males have flowers like thick black snakes and the females have this fruit.' My grandfather picks up the coco-de-mer, grunting with the effort. He shakes it so that I can hear the liquid moving inside. I imagine Eve climbing naked up a palm tree to grapple with this image of her own body, but maybe the nut was ripe and it simply dropped down beside her, breaking open where it fell. My grandfather rubs it with the corner of his sleeve and then puts it back in its place next to the other things.

'General Gordon stayed with us for several weeks,' he says. 'He wrote an article for a magazine in which he explained that he had found Paradise, but unfortunately I have lost the article. I sat on his knee and he smoked a pipe, but I can't remember him, I was much too young.'

I pick up the piece of red coral that is as hard and smooth as a tooth. 'Is this from Praslin as well?' I say.

'Coral,' he says, and snatches it from my hand as if he thought I might steal it. 'We are protected by a fence of coral all around the island, although much of it has been broken away now. And this is a snail shell which I used to keep in my pocket for a while and this is a crucifix which my father gave me, and this is a land crab's claw but not a very big one. We have lots of giant land crabs here and they are like red hands with fat hairy fingers crawling up the trunks of trees and clacking their shells together. We used to have giant tortoises,

but that was long ago, although we still have green turtles and black parrots and the white tropic birds with
this long tail feather that made me think of angels.
And hurricanes that try to break all the trees and
sweep away the houses and hundreds of black sea slugs
in the shallow water and a church bell thanks to my
father who was a missionary as you probably know. You
see, when I was a child there were no white people here
apart from Mr and Mrs Penbury who seemed to have
arrived by mistake, but there were lots of black men
and women and children and the witch-doctors were
very powerful which was why my father had come to
stamp them out along with all their wickedness. The
witch-doctors could make you blind even though
there was nothing wrong with your eyes. They could
kill you if they wanted to, or put a long curse on you
which passes from one member of the family to the
next. That's very hard to shake off. Very hard. Very
hard', and my grandfather seems to be falling asleep,
his head nodding forward, his eyes closed.

But suddenly he is awake again. He leans forward
and picks up the crucifix on a chain and hangs it
around his neck. Then he picks up the little tin and
places it in the flat of his hand. 'Do you see this?' he
says, and he taps at the lid with the tip of his finger.
'This is filled with a powder. Evalina gave it to me,
although perhaps you don't know Evalina. It's made

from menstrual blood and semen mixed together and heated over a fire until it's ready.' He carefully removes the lid of the tin and inside I can see a little heap of grey powder. It smells musty and strangely familiar. He dips his finger into the powder and then licks it off with a pink tongue. He clears his throat and rubs his hands together so that they make a dry rustling sound like snakes in a box.

# Seven

My grandfather puts the lid on the little tin and snaps it shut and then he packs all his treasures back into the wooden box. The coco-de-mer gleams and glistens. It looks like an egg that might break open to reveal some wonderful mythical beast. He strokes it as if it was a living thing in need of comfort and there is an expression of unexpected tenderness on his face. He stares at the blank wooden wall in front of him and he seems to be watching images that move. He starts to weep: two thin lines of tears running down his cheeks.

'He is remembering his childhood,' says the pig and I had quite forgotten that the pig was still here with me.

On the wall there is a picture of the house that we are in; it's a low white-painted building with a long veranda, standing on sand and among trees and next to it is what must be a church. Both buildings shimmer in the bright sunlight like mirages.

'Look,' says my grandfather. Close to the house he has caught a glimpse of a man with his arm in a sling and the man frightens him although he is not sure why. And there is Evalina Larose who used to live with them although he never knew if she was a servant or a distant relative. She has thin legs and a solid body, big flat teeth, cool hands and a singing voice that would creep step by step down his spine.

He walks away from the house and enters the forest of the Valley of May. He is surrounded by hundreds of palm trees, their scaly trunks moving and creaking in the wind, and other trees with huge bespread leaves, the sun shining through the leaves as if through coloured glass in a church window. There is the smell of growth all around him and when he stands very still he can see the spikes of new shoots pushing up through the soil as fast as the dragon's teeth in the fairy story. He can hear each leaf uncurl with a clatter as it shakes itself free from a dried husk or the casing of a shell.

He can run. My grandfather can run like the wind. He can race along the white sand of the beach and clouds of birds fly up into the sky just ahead of him. Usually he manages to be alone but sometimes his father is there as well, red-faced and dangerous, carrying the gun that he carried wherever he went except when he was entering a church or a house. His father lifts the gun and shoots at the birds so that one or

perhaps many of them fall in a swoon at his feet. Once
he shoots a snake and the boy watches as the force of
the bullet makes it spring into the air, scattering its
broken flesh. His father takes the dead snake and nails
it to a tree, saying that will show the people how the
devil can be defeated.

My grandfather often thinks about the devil. All
his life he has been thinking about the devil. There are
she-devils as well of course, but usually he sees a black
man with a pink tongue, pink fingernails, and the soles
of his feet and the palms of his hands are pink as well.
His sex hangs between his thighs even darker than his
skin, like the flowers of the coco-de-mer or like those
sea slugs that drift and roll in the clear shallow water
around the island. There are always dozens of them
stranded along the beach, drying helplessly in the sun.
He never dared to pick one up but he did once ask
Evalina what they were and where they came from.
Evalina laughed until her teeth frightened him and she
said that his father the missionary had cut them from
the bodies of all the wicked fornicators and thrown
them into the sea.

'But they don't stay in the sea,' she said. 'After dark
they all come creeping back to where they belong.
Even the ones that look as if they are dead creep back.
If you went out at night you would see them with your
big black eyes.'

The spell of memory is broken. I'm not sure why,

maybe there was a sudden noise outside which brought us all back. My grandfather is still sitting on the floor in the corner of this room that he knew when he was a child and the pig and I are still with him; we have been watching him as he walks through the forest of palm trees and runs along the beach where the birds are flying. We heard him talking to Evalina and we heard Evalina answering him, teasing him about the sea slugs.

And then the door opens and in she comes. I recognise her at once from the thin legs, the solid body and the big teeth. She is carrying a chicken under her arm, a look of extreme surprise in its round eyes. She pulls out a chair and sits down facing us but she doesn't seem to see any of us and I don't think she would hear us if we tried to speak to her. With a simple quick movement she breaks the chicken's neck and lays its body on her lap, the head dangling over her bare knees, the bound feet so waxy and yellow. She begins to pluck the white feathers which fall around her like snow.

'It looks like snow,' says my grandfather in a shaky voice. 'I don't want to be here. I don't belong here. I want to go away.'

'He wants to leave Praslin,' says the pig very quietly. 'He wants to go somewhere where no one knows anything about him or his family. He wants to become an Englishman walking through a rose garden on a chilly afternoon with a mist rising from the river and the cold eating into his bones, numbing his flesh. But he can't go yet; he's got to stay here for a while.'

# Eight

I look into the pig's eyes and for the first time I notice that there are little gold flecks floating within the icy water of the iris. The eyelashes are almost orange. I used to keep pigs once and they would go for walks with me across the bleak fields; stopping when I stopped, running when I ran, stuffing their noses into the muddy earth in search of roots, pebbles, worms, beetles and anything else that they could find.

'Quick,' says the pig. 'Here comes the man with his arm in a sling. Ask your grandfather to tell you about the pig-faced man.'

'Will you tell me the story of the pig-faced man, Grandfather?' I say obediently.

'No, I won't,' he replies. 'It's none of your business. It's nobody's business except mine and anyway I have forgotten all about it.'

'But he's there, Grandfather,' I say, because it's true. 'Can't you see his face framed by the curtains? He's holding something up to show you, it looks like a wooden doll with a string of chilli peppers tied around its neck. I think he wants to climb in through the window, angry and naked with his arm in a sling. Who is he and why is he so angry?'

My grandfather fumbles in the wooden box and here again is the tin of powder and the silver crucifix. He sprinkles a thin line of powder on the floor in front of where he is sitting and kisses the crucifix. The man outside the window disappears. The sea breathes in and out. A bird sings its electric song.

'I was very afraid of my father the missionary,' my grandfather says. 'He taught me to shake hands like a man, but he said my hands were as damp and flimsy as a girl's. "Grip!" he said. "Grip! Grip!" He told me I must stand in front of the mirror every morning and punch myself on the chin to remove the weakness he saw there. He said, "You should have taken my eyes, my hair, my skin, but like a fool you chose your mother's."

'Every evening after we had prayed together he would wash my face with a mixture of bleach and the juice of a lemon and then before I went to bed he would strap a bag of stones on to my back to protect me from the bad dreams that visit children when their faces are exposed to the night air. I would wake to feel the sharpness of the stones and the black night hovering over me. I had nightmares but I never dared to tell anyone about the things that visited me while I slept.

'My father had come to the island to stamp out

copulation. He often said so to my mother and to me, and, although I didn't know what the word meant, I knew he could do it if he wanted to. Then after Evalina had explained the word to me and told me about the sea slugs I used to imagine him going out secretly to collect them and trampling a whole nest of them under his feet. Evalina told me about the loup-garou, a werewolf who was disguised as a man during the day, and I began to think that this must be what happened to my father. He was so frightening, we were all frightened of him and sometimes I would lie awake at night and I could hear growling yelping noises coming from the room where he slept with my mother. I imagined him stepping into his hairy skin and I imagined the look of terror in my mother's eyes because she was there with him, sharing his secret.

'My father was usually very busy during the day. "He is looking for Christians," my mother used to say, as if he could find them under stones or hiding behind trees. Over the years he baptised quite a few men, women and children, but not as many as he would have wished because the witch-doctors were so strong and they did not like my father. "It's a battle between the powers of darkness and the powers of light," he said, and I imagined a struggle of bodies along the beach close to our house and the blood from the dead and wounded soaking into the sand and spreading across the surface of the water. "It's a battle between the powers of darkness and the powers of light," he said and he told me the story of the madman who lived among the tombstones in a cemetery and was so strong that no chains could hold him. Then Jesus came and threw his madness into a herd of pigs that went screaming over the edge of a cliff and were drowned in the sea. "But what had the pigs done wrong?" I asked him and regretted it at once because he hit me and said I was insolent.

'My father loved shooting. He said it was the only entertainment to be found on the island. He made a collection of the long white trailing tail feathers of the tropic birds that look like angels when they float across the sky. He shot the black parrots because they were rare and although there were no tortoises any more there were some big lizards and snakes and he shot them. And turtles, but it's hard to kill a turtle.

'So one day my father took me shooting with him. We had just entered the Valley of May when we heard a noise, a panting grunting sound that was neither entirely human nor entirely animal. "It's the devil!" shouted my father. "I've got him now!" and he rushed ahead, plunging through the trees with me following as fast as I could, my heart thumping in my head.

'I caught up with my father standing in a clearing in front of a wooden pen made out of the trunks of palm trees. He looked terrible because his face was red and sweating. He had already raised his gun and was taking aim and I looked into the pen and saw two figures on a bed of leaves: a naked man with the face of a pig and a naked woman who was half hidden under his crouching body, her face obscured by a mass of dark hair.

' "Devil!" shouted my father, and he shot the man in his right arm close to the elbow so that he lurched to his feet screaming with pain. In a moment he had clambered out of the pen and was running off into the camouflage of trees. The woman stood up with her back to me and her body was very beautiful, the skin the same colour as my mother's skin, and it was only then that I started to scream as if I was the one who had been shot. My father shook me and shook me until I was shaken into silence and the woman had gone and we went home.

'On the morning of the next day the man they called Bonhomme Michel came to our house with his arm in a sling. He was there staring in at the window and my mother saw him and let out a cry as if she had been shot as well. I think he meant to put a curse on my father but it fell on my mother instead. It happens like that sometimes.

'And now,' says my grandfather, 'I am very tired, so if you'll excuse me I would like to sleep', and without waiting for a reply he curls himself up on the floor, his head bent, his knees towards his chest. He looks so small and fragile lying there and as I watch I see him fading before my eyes; his body becomes colourless and transparent, the walls of the house around him are as thin as lace curtains and a wind is blowing in across the room, covering everything with a blanket of sand. Soon there will be nothing left; even the pig will have disappeared.

Part II

# Nine

The boy has been sleeping with his hand clenched under the small of his back so that the bag of stones won't hurt him, and now the hand is cramped and tingling. He holds it up in front of his face; he can just see it in the first light of the dawn and it looks like a crab; the fingers move like crab's legs.

He listens to the soft breath of the sea. He stares at the palm-leaf partition that separates this room from the room where his parents sleep. He can hear something rustling among the dried leaves. It might be a rat.

'It's only a rat!' that's what his father said when he found one lying dead by the front door on the day when Bonhomme Michel came visiting. 'It's only a rat, boy, don't cringe!' holding it by the tip of its grey snake tail and spinning it in the air before throwing it among the trees behind the house. The boy went to find it later and a swarm of flies had already settled on it, bringing it to life with their wriggling maggot babies.

'It was only a rat,' his mother said, sitting on the

edge of his bed in her white dress, her hand cool on his forehead. 'Don't be afraid, dodo, it can't hurt you, it's dead.' And she sang him one of the Creole songs that the people of the island like to sing; the one about the young man who is going to be married in the morning to the daughter of Madame Eugène, but everyone knows that Madame Eugène is a bad woman, so her daughter will be bad as well. Some of the words of the song had no meaning but they made a lovely sound, like birdsong:

> *Ela le la la*
> *Ela le lololo*
> *Elale le la e lololo*

It wasn't only the rat that died on the day when Bonhomme Michel came visiting, it was the cat as well. It came into the boy's room and crouched in a corner and he could tell at once that it was staring at death and the first one to blink or flinch was the one who had lost. He watched it shrug its shoulders, close its eyes and it was gone; all that was left was the limp body. He took it and buried it in the sand close to the sea and he made a cross out of two pieces of driftwood bound together with string. In spite of his fear he forced himself to go out into the night to pray on his knees in the darkness because that would give his cat a hope of heaven. He thought that one of those sea slugs went shuffling past quite close to him but he couldn't be sure.

But now something terrible has happened to the boy's mother and everything that has been familiar to him is suddenly becoming strange. The thoughts spin through his head so fast he cannot disentangle them from each other; they are like the mouse he once kept in a cage with a wheel for exercise and the wheel turning and turning day and night in a blur of movement.

He went with his mother to put some flowers in the church and when they came back there was that wooden doll with the string of chilli peppers around its neck, waiting for them on the doorstep. His mother bent down to examine it more closely and as she picked it up she let out a little cry as if she had been stung. She rushed to her bedroom and drew the curtains across the open windows so that the cloth seemed to be breathing in and out like the gills of a fish. She lay on the bed with the counterpane wrapped around her thin body and up to her chin and her eyes were wide open, just as the cat's had been. The boy sat beside her, not knowing what to do.

He might have been sitting there for a long time before his father came home with a clatter of hard shoes on the wooden floor, bursting into that quiet room with his dog-collar gleaming. He grabbed the boy's mother by her shoulders and almost lifted her out of the bed as he shook her with his red hands, just as he had shaken the boy when they were in the forest together, and her dark hair looked like that other woman's hair, it was also thick and wild.

'What is the matter? What has happened? What have they done?' and his father, who had always frightened him, shook his mother who was always frightened as if expecting her to drop her answers like ripe fruit. But she said nothing, she only smiled a vague and hopeless smile.

The boy wanted to get out of the room as soon as he could and he was standing a few paces back waiting for the right moment to escape when his father turned and saw him.

'What are you doing here? Get out, boy, get out at once! Are you deaf? Get out!' and so he turned and ran into the bright air outside.

He sat in the shade of a palm tree near to the place where the cat was buried. He scooped up a handful of fine sand and let it trickle through his fingers. He picked up an empty crab shell and crushed it in his fist. He could see the window of his parents' bedroom and the white curtains pulsating and it was as if he could see through the walls to where his mother was lying on the bed in the dim light. The blank stare of her dark eyes.

'You have my eyes,' she had said to him once. 'My poor dodo, I am sorry.'

# Ten

It was Evalina Larose who gave the boy the tin
of musty powder. She pressed it into his hand
and said that she would explain to him later what it
was, but for the moment he must keep it safe. She told
him that his mother had been cursed by Bonhomme
Michel. She said she was sure the curse had been
meant for his father but perhaps his father's anger had
been too strong or perhaps he was protected by the
power of his religion; anyway the curse had bounced
off him and struck his wife instead, like a stone that
you throw against a wall and it bounces back and hits
someone who happens to be standing close by. She
said that once a curse had taken root it always tried to
stay within a family and it can be passed down
through the generations from parents to their children and their grandchildren, just like a clock or a
gold ring, or an empty house. She said, 'You must
wear the crucifix your father gave you and when you

say your prayers put some of the powder on the tip of your tongue.'

Throughout that day the boy was forbidden to enter his mother's room, but he prayed for her when night came. The powder tasted strange but not unpleasant. He closed his eyes and he could see a mountain of clouds as if a storm was coming and there were angels moving among them, darting in and out like birds. He tried to find God but he couldn't find him anywhere and when he pressed the tips of his fingers into his closed eyes he was surrounded by a black sky with spinning stars and planets, red and green. No one heard him going back into his own room; he opened and closed the doors without making a sound.

His mother was not better by the morning. He crept into her room and there were dark greasy rings around her eyes and she wouldn't speak to him, she wouldn't even look at him. When he stood there in front of her he felt as though he no longer existed; he was nothing more than his own racing heartbeat. He went to find Evalina and she told him that his father had set off very early to fetch a doctor from the neighbouring island of Mahé.

'Not much a doctor can do,' said Evalina. She was in the kitchen with a big saucepan bubbling on the fire, filled with little snails of a sort the boy had never seen before. He peered at them through the steam and their bodies were all stretched out full length in the water as if they were trying to escape from their own shells. The boiling water made them jostle against each other, rattling softly. Evalina stirred them with a fork.

'Your father asks me to make snail water,' she said. 'Your father tells me that old Mrs Penbury was cured with snail water when her blood got too hot. She keeps a whole lot of these snails in a tin filled with bran because they don't come from this island, they come from Mauritius. Your father fetched them before he went.' And she held the shells and the escaping bodies back with her fork while she poured a grey frothing liquid into a jug.

She had another saucepan as well. It contained a mound of white crystals with a fragment of chilli pepper balanced on top, just like the drop of red blood in the snow that the boy had seen in a book of fairy stories.

'Now that your poor mother has been cursed,' said Evalina, 'I do what I can. I make an eye against an eye. I hope to do it quickly before your father comes home because he doesn't understand such things.'

She held the saucepan over the flames and the sharp smell of camphor filled the kitchen, crawling around the boy's eyes, down his throat, into his nostrils. 'Look!' said Evalina and blinking back the tears he looked into the saucepan and saw that the heap of crystals and the piece of chilli had turned themselves into a wicked eye with a burnt black pupil and a blood-red iris within a white island of powder.

Evalina led the way into the bedroom. The air here was sour and stale even though the window was open, but as soon as she entered with her jug and her saucepan the boy could feel how the smell of the camphor began to do battle with Bonhomme Michel's curse, his pig's face and his wounded arm. The boy was sure that this would make his mother better. It was a battle between the powers of darkness and the powers of light.

Her head was propped up on a pillow and her hair was spread out around her like a fan. 'Ah, there you are,' she said, but it didn't sound like her real voice, it was as if someone else was speaking from within her body.

She looked at the boy and at Evalina. She looked at the steaming jug and the saucepan. She sniffed the air and wrinkled her nose. 'Oh God, I am so unhappy!' she said and she began to laugh until her eyes were bright with her own laughter.

# Eleven

The boy wanted to forget what happened next on that day: how his mother laughed as she climbed down from the bed, her hair wild and bedraggled, her face damp. She was holding the hem of her nightdress in one hand and she moved with an exaggerated swaying of her hips, she moved like a dancer. 'I cannot bear to see these women dance,' his father had said, 'they dance like animals.'

His mother went up to Evalina and hugged her, twisting her thin arms around her and kissing her on the neck. Then she took a few wavering steps towards him. 'Come here my little one, my sweetheart,' she said in a mocking voice, 'come here my child of the island', and suddenly she lunged at him, grasping hold of him and wrapping him into the smell of cold sweat and the musty sourness of her. She was crying as well as laughing as she pressed him close against her body, her skin slippery, her bones sharp.

Then with the same passion with which she had
held him she flung him away so that he staggered and
would have fallen had not Evalina caught him and
steadied him. 'Don't worry,' said Evalina, 'it's burning
through. Let her burn it through and then she can be
herself again. We mustn't stop her. Let her burn.'

The boy was suddenly aware of his mother standing right in front of him. 'Look at me!' she was saying.
'Look how dirty I am! Look at my dirty flesh!' pulling
her long nightdress up over her head so that her arms
and face were bundled into whiteness and her thin
body seemed to dangle beneath it: the dark nipples, the
dark armpits, the dark triangle of her sex, the skin
gleaming like the fruit of the coco-de-mer.

And that was when his father arrived, flinging
open the door and bursting into the room like a dog
that is going to spring at the throat of an intruder. If a
gun had been in his hand he would not have paused
before shooting the she-devil who had entered his
house. He would have shot her and then maybe she
would have fallen back into her familiar shape and this
strange creature would have dropped from her and
lain dead on the floor.

The doctor was there as well. He was a tall man
with spectacles who was quick to decide what to do. He
pulled the counterpane from the bed and captured the
woman in it, wrapping her up like a bird in a net and

only then removing the nightdress that was hiding her face.

She stood there making a strange moaning sound and the boy wished that someone would hold her because he was sure she was going to hurt herself. He had to struggle for his own breath, he felt as if he was drowning and the water would soon close over his head. He was no longer able to distinguish between himself and the people who were in the room with him; he seemed to have become all of them at once. He was his own father shaking with rage, he was his mother wrapped in a counterpane, he was the doctor sitting straight-backed in a chair with his black medical bag open on his lap, he was Evalina slumped against the wall; he was even the house that held them and the windows that looked out towards the sea.

That night he was taken to stay with Mr and Mrs Penbury who kept snails in a tin and were the only other white family on the island. They seemed embarrassed and did not want to talk to him. On the following morning the doctor came and took him to the island of Mahé and he remained there for two weeks at least, although it could have been much longer since he lost count of the days. The doctor lived on his own but he was a very busy man and the boy hardly ever saw him. A maid came to clean the house and prepare food and there was a big orange cat with green eyes which liked to sleep during the day but went out hunting and crying for companionship at night. When the boy stroked the cat it would roll on to its back and grasp his hand with its claws, biting at his skin with sharp teeth and even drawing blood. He learnt to wrap his hand in a cloth so that he could challenge it to attack him again and again.

He was playing with the cat when his father came to collect him. He was suddenly there towering above him, holding out his land crab of a hand by way of a greeting, and the boy was so startled and surprised that he struggled to his feet and held out his hand to be shaken within its covering of torn cloth.

'Well, my boy,' said his father once they had disentangled themselves. 'Expect you'd like to see your mother? And she's looking forward to seeing you. But I should tell you that she has been ill so you must be careful not to upset her; make sure you don't talk about anything that has happened. You see, your mother has shown herself to be susceptible to the powers of darkness, although luckily you don't yet know what that means. She will need to go to hospital, but hospitals are very good at dealing with such problems. So come along, let's be on our way.'

When the boy met his mother again she was much smaller and older than he had remembered her as being. Her hair was pulled back from her face and she was wearing a grey dress that was different from any of the clothes she used to wear.

'Hello, my dear,' she said, gazing at him with a vague curiosity but not seeming to recognise him. Her voice was tremulous and she had powdered her face and neck with a white powder that smelled of unfamiliar flowers.

'We are going to leave Praslin,' she said absent-mindedly. 'Just you and me and Evalina. Father will join us when he can. We are going to Mauritius, the land of the dodo. You will like it, there are monkeys in the forest. Now give your poor mother a kiss and tell her how glad you are to see her again after your holiday.'

# Twelve

And so they set off, Evalina, the boy and his mother, leaving the island of Praslin and heading for the island of Mauritius. The journey on a French cargo ship takes about ten days. The three of them share a cabin with two bunk-beds for the women and a thin mattress on the floor for the boy. At night Evalina sleeps on her back snoring rhythmically with her mouth open. Nothing wakes her, not even the sound of the boy's mother who often whimpers like a dog that has been shut out and wants to be let in.

There is a single porthole in the cabin and when the boy lies on his mattress he can see the clear expanse of the night sky flecked with stars or diluted by the moon. The gentle rocking and creaking of the boat makes him feel as if he is inside a living creature, but although he is repeatedly lulled to the edge of sleep he is unable to fall into it and always shudders back into wakefulness. The hours go by and he keeps very

still, the porthole staring at him with a single unblink-
ing eye.

His father had come with them as far as the island
of Mahé. He supervised the loading of their luggage on
to the boat and stood beside them on the deck, a pan-
ama hat shielding the redness of his face, the dog-
collar looking tight and uncomfortable in the heat.
When the ship's horn sounded the time for him to
depart he clasped his thin wife in his arms and kissed
her on the mouth which the boy had never seen him
do before. She let out the same startled cry she had
made when she picked up the wooden doll on the steps
of their house and the boy thought that she might run
blindly over the side of the ship, but she held on to the
passenger rail and didn't move.

His father said, 'Goodbye, my boy, I'm sure it's for
the best', and he gripped his son's hand and smiled so
that for the first and last time the boy had a glimpse of
the sadness in him. He took Evalina to one side and
spoke to her in a low whispered voice and then suddenly he was off, racing down the gangplank just
before it was lifted, pushing through a crowd of
bystanders on the quay and striding out of sight without once turning round to wave. The boy watched his
father's shoulders retreating. His fingers were tingling
and he rubbed the moist palm against his shirt sleeve
before stuffing his hand into the pocket of his shorts. In

the pocket he found a snail shell and he stroked its spiral pattern with his thumb.

His mother was standing next to him. She took out her powder compact and opened it so that the mirror glinted in the sun. She dabbed so much of the powder on her face that it looked as if she had tripped and fallen into a bowl of flour. The boy thought she looked like a ghost.

'Well, that's over and done with,' she said, closing the powder compact with a snap and putting it back in her bag. She smiled a wide blank smile that the boy had never seen before, and she said, 'Now that your father has gone you can tell me the truth. Am I dead? I think I must be but I want to be sure. Am I dead?'

The boy didn't know what to reply. His mouth was dry. He gazed out at the distant line of the horizon and the glassy calm of the sea stretching towards it. He looked down into the water where a shoal of silver fishes twisted and turned with flashes of light. Below them he could just distinguish the dark shapes of the sea slugs and those strange worms called venus girdles that look like long coils of brown rope, but are so soft you can hardly tell if you are touching them. If you try to pick one up it slides through your fingers like jelly. He hoped his mother wouldn't ask him any more difficult questions.

'If you won't speak to me then Evalina will be more

friendly,' she said at last. 'She will know how to look after me, although really I don't need to worry because nothing bad can happen to the dead. Come on, let's go and find Evalina and ask her to play cards.'

And so the three of them played cards together. At all times of the day they played cards, sitting around a little collapsible table with a green baize top, a canvas awning to give them shade and the sea so solid and quiet that the ship hardly disturbed the water as it moved forward. 'It's as if we were being pulled by a rope,' said the boy, but no one heard him.

Their favourite game was vingt-et-un. They all placed bets and concentrated very hard. They didn't use money, but Evalina had a pile of well-ironed hand-kerchiefs that were all given the same value, while the boy had his wooden box filled with treasures and each item had a different value, starting with the shell that had been in his pocket and going up to the little tin filled with musty powder. He could have used the coco-de-mer as well since he had it in one of his suit-cases, but it would have been too heavy and cumber-some and it might easily have rolled into the sea.

His mother played for more abstract things. For each new game she would tear pieces of blank paper out of her notebook and say with great authority, 'This is a husband. This is an immortal soul. This is a tea party. This is a man or it might be a pig, I'm not sure, but anyway it's worth six points.' She made tiny indecipherable marks on the papers as she set them down and never forgot what each one represented.

At the end of the game they would all reclaim their possessions. Evalina folded up her handkerchiefs and tucked them into the front of her dress, the boy returned his treasures to their box. But his mother tore her paper into little pieces and scattered them over the side of the ship.

Time passed and the days moved on. An albatross followed them for several hours, its crooked shadow wavering and flapping on the deck. They saw dolphins in the distance and something which might have been a whale. The sunsets were very beautiful and so were the dawns. The boy's mother trailed her finger in a splash of sea water on the passenger rail. She put her finger in her mouth. 'It tastes like blood,' she said and smiled one of those wide blank smiles.

She ate very little, moving the food from one side of her plate to the other, tapping at it with her knife, bringing a laden fork to her lips and then putting it down untasted as if she had something important to say at that moment. She went to bed early and got up late and she often fell asleep in her chair on the deck under the canvas awning. She would fall asleep abruptly and without warning, as if a switch had been pulled, severing her connection with the waking world. She was always afraid when she woke and so the boy and Evalina took it in turns to sit with her.

At night, when his mother was already flickering through her sleep, Evalina would sometimes talk to the boy, telling him stories in the darkness.

# Thirteen

T he boy closes his eyes and Evalina's soft voice enters his head and takes up residence there. 'Your father has arranged everything,' she says. 'Your mother will go to a hospital where they will try to shake her out of her trouble, although I don't know what good that will do. You can shake and shake but nothing changes and she will still have Bonhomme Michel's teeth in her neck, won't she? But that's how it is. I will go to Black River where I have family and you will go to your Uncle Julius. He lives at Chamarel in a house near the waterfall up in the mountains with high trees all around. He looks like your father with a red face and big hands and he gets angry just like your father does so you must be careful. I remember he used to have a fruit bat that hung on the back of his chair in the dining-room and it always unwrapped its wings and called out to him when he entered the room. I wonder if it's still with him. It's many years since I was last there; your father and mother met each other in that house.'

Evalina is silent and in the silence the boy feels as if his body has deserted him and he is nothing more than a speck of dust drifting within an immensity that has no boundaries. Then Evalina says, 'I remember the trees around your uncle's house, so tall and thick that they shut out the sky, and there were monkeys in the branches with the faces of old men and old women. Sometimes they would climb on to the veranda and sit there chattering together with their shoulders hunched, but you have never seen a monkey, have you?'

'No,' says the boy, 'never', and the sound of his own voice startles him.

Evalina says, 'That forest is so noisy. There are the birds, the animals, the insects, the lizards, but no snakes which is lucky; and there are also the other creatures: the zombies, the ghosts, the loup-garou, because the forest is their home as well. Many of the trees near the house are the bodies of slaves who worked for your uncle's family and were turned into zombies after they had died. At night I have seen them shake themselves free from the soil and then go walking as quiet as shadows. They have bark as smooth as your skin: the black-skinned ebony, the white-skinned applewood tree, the *makak*, the *tamabacoque*. You can recognise the zombies at once because they look like men or women with their heads hidden in the earth and their arms holding on as roots; their naked bodies stretching up and dividing into long legs. You will see.'

'But how is a zombie made?' asks the boy, although he seems to know already. He can feel them moving and breathing all around him, a whole crowd of them just out of reach of his hand.

'A zombie is someone who has died before they were ready to leave the world, and that is why a sorcerer is able to pull them back into life after they are dead. They are not always turned into trees; some of them look like ordinary people but they stare at you with glassy eyes and they don't need to blink. Their voices are different as well, they have slow tired voices and seem to be speaking from inside a box. They are often treated very badly but they never cry out or complain because they have forgotten who they are, but I have been told that if they get a taste of salt then they go mad with despair and can be dangerous.'

'And have you known anyone who was turned into a zombie?' asks the boy.

'Oh yes,' says Evalina. 'There was a girl who was the same age as me, we were like sisters. She had mixed blood although you couldn't see it on her face and she fell in love with a man who was white. He was going to marry her until somebody told him that her grandmother had been a black slave, and when he knew the truth there was nothing she could do and so she killed herself. We buried her in a cemetery close to the sea with a metal railing around the grave, but a few weeks later she came back from the dead. Her parents saw her walking along the main street of the town in a red dress. She didn't recognise them because she had no memory and when they called her she ran away and hid, but they caught her in the end. She was too wild and strange to be kept at home, so she was taken to a hospital where the nuns looked after her.'

'And did she get better?' asks the boy, who is thinking of his mother now.

'I don't know,' says Evalina. 'I went to visit her once in the hospital: long corridors and my feet clicking on those hard floors. She was all on her own in a room with no furniture except the bed and she never moved, she just stared at the ceiling. A sorcerer would have been more help to her than the nuns. The sorcerer who lived at Black River told me that we should have buried her with her face pressed against the earth, a dagger in her hand and her mouth sewn up with thread; so that she couldn't answer if anyone called her and she could fight if someone tried to force her to her feet. The sorcerer said I could bring her to him to see if he could undo the spell, but there were locked gates and high fences all around the hospital.'

'Evalina,' says the boy, 'is my mother a zombie? Has she died because of Bonhomme Michel's curse and is that why she has changed so much?'

'I suppose she has in a way,' says Evalina in a dreamy voice as if she was on the edge of sleep. 'She might come back or she might not come back; she is trapped, if you know what I mean. But you must be very careful now. You must use that powder I gave you whenever you see Bonhomme Michel or someone who makes you think of Bonhomme Michel. Wear the crucifix as well at such times. Be on guard.'

'Can't we go to the sorcerer who lives at Black River?' asks the boy, but Evalina is already asleep. The moon has risen and he can see it peering in through the porthole. His mother whimpers in the darkness and tosses her body restlessly from side to side. The boy tries to remember what Bonhomme Michel looked like and suddenly he can see him very clearly, standing there in front of him with one arm in a sling.

# Fourteen

The sea is always calm, the nights are hot, the days are long. The boy feels as if he has forgotten what it was like to live on Praslin; everything seems to have drifted away from him out of the reach of memory. He sometimes wonders if this is what it's like to be dead, cut loose from the world. His father once told him that the souls of the dead have to go on a long journey and he always imagined them naked in a little boat, peering into the distance with worried eyes.

Evalina says that the island they are going to is very different from the island they have left behind. 'There are high mountains,' she says, 'higher than the clouds, and you can get completely lost among them. You can walk for hours and hours without ever catching a glimpse of the sea. There are towns and villages, roads and railway lines and crowds of people you have never seen before and will never see again. The people are as numerous as ants in an ant nest, there are more of them than you would ever believe possible. When we arrive at Port Louis you will be afraid of all those faces, the noise, the smell, the crowds pushing against you. Then you must keep hold of my hand and your mother's hand as well. We must not be separated.

'I hope your uncle will come to meet us at the dock. He owns a sugar plantation called Mon Plaisir and he is very rich because of all that sugar, you can see it in the way he dresses and the way that people obey him. His house is so big you might never see all the rooms it contains, and the garden is full of zozo birds, or at least it was when I was there. You will like the zozos; if you flutter a white handkerchief they come flying out of the bushes to land on your head and shoulders. They are so tiny you can't feel the weight of their bodies, only the prick of their sharp feet.'

'Zozo birds,' says the boy, enjoying the unexpected sound.

'Zozo,' says his mother who he had thought was asleep. 'Zozo, zozo, dors petit zozo, dors.'

'But first we will stay in Port Louis for a few days,' says Evalina. 'We might go to the market. It has a big metal gate decorated with Queen Victoria's crown and the letters V.R. But never let go of my hand in the market or someone might grab hold of you and sell you from a market stall. They sell brightly-coloured birds brought over from Africa, big parrots with grey tongues and monkeys and flying foxes and rats which only the poor people eat. Your father told me that last year your uncle killed forty thousand rats on his estate. That's how rich he is.'

'I don't like rats,' says the boy's mother who is sitting up in her bunk-bed now, her hands folded together as if in prayer. 'I saw that dead rat and I said "Don't be afraid, it's dead, it can't hurt you." But that wasn't true, was it? All kinds of things can hurt.'

'We might go to the museum in Port Louis,' says Evalina to the boy as if she hadn't heard the talk about the rat. 'They have all the birds, all the fishes, all the animals you could ever see: three lovely rooms full of them. They have a giant tortoise big enough to carry five men on its back and the dodo that hasn't existed for more than a hundred years. A man found it in the marsh that is called La Mare aux Songes, the Pool of Dreams. Everybody was very excited. They were draining the land to get the peat and there was the dodo, its beak, its feathers, everything in perfect condition, but it needed to be carefully cleaned. They also found lots of bones; it seems that hundreds of dodos had gone to die there although no one knew why.'

'I know why,' says the boy's mother very quietly. 'The dodos went to the Pool of Dreams because they were lonely and wanted to be all of them together in the cold water.'

# Fifteen

It's very early in the morning when the boat approaches the island of Mauritius. The air is still cold and the dawn is streaking the grey sky with the colour of apricots. The boy stands shivering and alone on the deck and he can see what must be a range of mountains, like the wings of a huge bird, or the wings of Satan, leathery and creaking in the wind. Against the darkness of the mountains he can just distinguish thin columns of white smoke rising up and fading into a mist. A pair of tropic birds are flying overhead and he is glad for the familiarity of their long trailing tail feathers.

The boat pulls closer to the shore as the dawn grows stronger. He realises that what he had imagined to be a clutter of dark stone at the foot of the mountains is in fact houses, hundreds of buildings containing thousands of people. And there on the quay he can see the people; not like ants as Evalina had said, but more like the maggots that appeared out of nowhere on the body of the dead rat. As he watches he feels a new sort of fear tumbling down his throat.

Evalina is standing next to him now and his mother is on the deck as well, leaning against the passenger rail and staring down into the sea. She is wearing a white dress and a hat made from feathers with a white veil that conceals her face. She is smiling with some private thought and the boy can just distinguish her teeth under the lace. She looks up at him and says, 'I must protect my skin from the sun. That's what they all tell us to do, isn't it, my little zozo?'

The side of the boat is bumping against the side of the quay and the crowd that has been waiting for this moment of connection ripples with excitement. Nothing that Evalina had said could have prepared the boy for such a crowd. He had not understood that there could ever be so many strangers in the world. There is a rich musty smell in the air: spices and bodies, fruit and meat and excrement and a roar of noise like a gathering storm.

'Where is that uncle of yours?' says Evalina. 'Can you see a man who looks like your father?'

But the boy cannot see anyone who looks like anyone.

A triangle of white steps is pushed against the side of the boat and the passengers begin to disembark. The boy is held by Evalina's hand which grips him as tight as a claw and he holds his mother's hand which is limp and delicate. The three of them walk carefully down the steps and on to the land. At first the boy can still feel the sea breathing heavily under his feet, but that sensation soon passes and the ground becomes solid and motionless.

Just as they are about to enter a big shed where their luggage has been taken, they see a man who is working his way towards them through the crowd. 'There is your Uncle Julius,' announces Evalina triumphantly. The boy looks up at the approaching figure and is confronted by a replica of his own father but terribly aged, the body thick and heavy, tight within the containment of a pale suit as if it would soon split the cloth open. The red skin of this man's face is crisscrossed with deep lines, the eyes look bruised, and yet he is so much like the boy's father that it is as if the journey on the boat must have lasted for many years and now the two of them are meeting again after a long absence.

'Evalina. My dear. Boy,' says the man as he glances briefly at each of them in turn. He sounds like the boy's father as well, but his voice is more thick and slow as if it had to push its way through a layer of mud.

'Carriage waiting. Hotel Universe. Luggage follows, seen to that,' and he shoos them forward like sheep until they reach a carriage which is more of a cart and they climb in.

Now they are bumping into the town. The boy's mother's hand has woken up and is stroking his palm with light fingers. The man who is not his father sits facing him and there is no glimmer of recognition in his eyes. The streets are all very straight with paved walks and open sewers running along the sides of them. Some of the houses are built from huge beams of wood with delicately carved doorways and wooden tiles on the roofs. The long verandas are covered with a mass of trailing creepers and bright flowers but the wooden blinds across the verandas are mostly drawn down so that the houses appear to be fast asleep. The boy sees a dog lying on its side with its head lolling on to the street, the white fur worn away to reveal patches of pink skin underneath. He sees the silhouettes of two cats on a roof. He sees brightly coloured birds in tiny cages hanging from hooks like fruit on a tree. He sees a monkey in a cage that is hardly bigger than its own body and it seems to catch his eye as they judder past so that he cries out with its despair.

'What was that?' says Uncle Julius, looking at the boy with unexpected fierceness.

'Nothing,' says the boy, 'it was only a monkey.'

His mother giggles and squeezes his fingers.

They turn off into a narrow dirty street. A beggar is

blocking their way. He has a turban wrapped around his head and a cloth tied around his waist and his arms and legs are insect thin. Suddenly he springs to one side with surprising agility and as they pass he makes a low sweeping bow.

'Who was that?' asks the boy, although he had meant to keep silent.

'Nobody,' replies Uncle Julius and he blows his nose loudly into a white handkerchief.

The carriage has come to a halt in front of a wooden two-storey building. The words Hotel Universe are written in curly black letters on a green board above the veranda.

'Come along,' says Uncle Julius, grasping the boy's shoulder just as his father might have done. 'This is where you are for the next few days before we set off to Chamarel', and he leads the way up the steps of the veranda, through a door and along a dark narrow corridor. They pass a room in which three men are playing a game of billiards, the ivory balls clicking together, but no one looks up or speaks.

They enter a wide, damp-smelling room with three little beds in it and the thin strips of light that permeate the shutters make the room seem as if it is behind bars. Apart from the beds, there are a table, a chair, a washstand and a mirror on the wall set in an ornate gold frame.

'Well, is there anything you need to know?' asks Uncle Julius, standing very large in front of the shuttered window, the side of his head reflected in the mirror so that it looks like a strange painting. 'I must be off now to do business. Your luggage will arrive soon and we meet on Wednesday, in the morning, ten o'clock. You can eat here. Explore the town. Evalina knows her way about and so do you, my dear', and he turns towards the boy's mother who looks away, to avoid him.

'Have you still got the fruit bat?' asks the boy, who had remembered the story of the bat when he saw the little chair in this room.

'Did your mother tell you about him?' says Uncle Julius and he smiles so that a new set of lines appears around his mouth and under his eyes. 'Not that one, but another one the same. Only you must be careful because he bites. The other one could be vicious as well, couldn't he, my dear?'

But the boy's mother does not answer; she is examining the tips of her fingers one by one. Uncle Julius claps his hands together, shrugs his shoulders and picks up his walking stick which has a carved ivory duck's head to serve as a handle. 'Until Wednesday then,' he says and he is gone without closing the door behind him.

# Sixteen

The boy slept well that night in spite of the mosquitoes humming in his ear, the barking of a dog, the billiard balls clicking against each other, two men shouting and a woman crying.

He woke to the sound of people talking in the street immediately outside the window and for a moment he listened and sniffed the air with no recollection of where he might be. He almost did not know who he was either, his mind caught on the image of the woman who was no longer his mother and the man who seemed to be his father grown prematurely old.

He stared through the partial darkness of the room and there was Evalina sitting in front of the mirror and brushing her hair so that it stood out very thick and black. And there was his mother lying on her back on a narrow bed. It looked as though she was nothing more than her own face, a naked disembodied face on a pillow like the head of John the Baptist on the dish.

The boy could suddenly imagine jellyfish with human faces, drifts of them floating across the ocean, all singing together, their mouths moving in perfect unison. He could see the tangled knot of tentacles beneath each one, as if that was the wound where the body had been hacked away.

'We'll go to the museum today,' said Evalina, and at the sound of her voice the jellyfish disappeared without trace.

The boy's mother was awake. 'I had such a funny dream,' she said. 'I dreamt that the three of us were on a boat for days and days, with nothing to do except play cards and stare at the sea. And when we arrived at the place we were going to, my husband came to meet me, but he had turned into an old man with a bright red face. Then I realised that he was dead and I was dead and we were all dead. Oh zozo!'

She began to cry and Evalina went to comfort her and to help her put on her clothes, while the boy dressed himself and then sat and gazed into the mirror until his dark eyes gazed back at him with a look of vague surprise.

They drank coffee and ate bread and jam in an enclosed courtyard with plants in big clay pots on a tiled floor and a crooked fig tree growing from a square of exposed earth in the centre of the courtyard. The walls were painted lime green and the paint was blis-

tered and flaky. A little girl came to watch them with a
kitten clasped tightly in her arms. The waiter spoke
only in a patois that the boy could not understand,
although some of the words sounded familiar. His
mother remained silent and Evalina did all the talking.

The museum was not far away. They went out of
the hotel and past a shop with bales of brightly
coloured silk heaped up in the window, past a shop
which sold sacks of sugar, a shop where they made pots
and pans and watering cans out of tin, a stall where a
tiny Chinaman was selling pieces of pineapple dipped
in a red sauce and a butcher's shop with strips of meat
and offal hanging dangerously from hooks. There were
crowds of people moving in all directions and beggars
sitting very still, stretching out their empty hands as
the boy walked by.

'Look,' said Evalina, 'now we are coming to the
museum.' The boy looked and he could see a row of
huge banyan trees with their branches trailing to the
ground, alive with the chattering of little birds that
were feeding among the branches. The pavement
beneath his feet was sticky with fallen fruit. Beyond the
trees there was a grass lawn which led to the steps of a
grand stone building. It seemed so serious and important that the boy held his breath as he walked up the
stone steps and in through the shining doors with their
gleaming brass handles.

The first room was filled with birds. There were the round staring eyes of hawks, clinging with sharp feet to dead branches; there was an albatross with its enormous wings stretched to their full span and a group of pigeons as pink as sugar mice. And all on its own in a glass case with a painted jungle and a bright blue painted sky, there was the poor dodo. The boy had never imagined how hopeless it would appear, a look of utter bewilderment on its face.

The next room was like an ocean. The walls were a milky blue and the floor shone like sunlight on a calm sea. A whale's skull was strapped down with metal bands on a wooden box as if it might otherwise thrash its way to freedom. The boy ran his fingers gently along the bone from the eye socket to the tip of the nose. Just above his head two big brown fishes swam from wires fixed to the ceiling, their mouths open in a quest for food, and in a far corner he could see several members of the shark family also hanging from wires. The violin shark was nothing like the picture he had been shown of a violin, but the hammer-headed shark did have a head that was shaped like a hammer with an eye on each blunt end. His favourites were the two shovel-nosed sharks, a little one poised close to the protective flank of a bigger one. When a breeze blew in from the gardens outside all these quiet creatures began to sway very gently and the boy felt as if he was on the bed of the ocean, looking up at their pale bellies and their strange lop-sided smiles.

In the next room there were some land animals in glass cases, but what drew the boy's attention were the giant tortoises and turtles. Six of them had been grouped together on the floor and they were as big as armchairs, gleaming a mahogany brown. It was the giant tortoise from Flat Island that attracted him most. It had a wise kind face filled with forgiveness and pity. It was smiling and its dark brown eyes seemed to be on the edge of tears. The boy wanted to sit on the floor next to it, to run his lips against the polished skull. He could almost see it breathing, blinking, opening its hard mouth to reveal a pink tongue. He felt that it understood the mystery of life and given time it might explain everything to him. But then his mother was there as well. She knelt in front of the tortoise, cupped her hands on either side of its face and kissed it on the mouth. 'My dear,' she said, 'here we are in the Pool of Dreams and I am so happy to see you again.'

# Seventeen

Uncle Julius came to collect them at nine o'clock in the morning, a little earlier than expected, and he was in a great hurry to get going. They were still in the courtyard finishing breakfast when he arrived, and after a brief greeting he went inside the hotel with Evalina 'to settle things,' he said.

When he emerged again into the daylight he sat down next to the boy and took hold of his hand. He smelt of overripe plums. 'I expect you know that your mother needs to go to hospital for a while,' he said, his face leaning closer so that the boy had to breathe through his open mouth to escape from the sweet, rotten smell. 'A very nice hospital, more like a hotel really', and he smiled across at the boy's mother who smiled back as if enjoying a shared secret. He seemed to be waiting for some sort of response to this information, but the boy had nothing to say. If he had been on a boat he would have stared down into the water hoping for the miracle of darting fishes, but here he only had the patterns and shapes made by the green paint flaking on the walls around him. He saw the profile of a man with a broken nose and a creature that would have been a tortoise but the legs were too long.

'You can write to her whenever you want to,' continued his uncle. 'I expect you can visit her once she has settled in. So if you'd like to say goodbye, Evalina and I will take her now and you can wait here. Have some more breakfast; you can have coffee, mangoes, cake, anything you choose. We'll be back in two hours and then we'll set off for my house in the mountains. But now my dear . . .' and he turned to the boy's mother . . . 'are you ready?'

'Oh yes,' she replied, 'I am ready. I am quite ready', and she took out her powder compact and powdered her face. She got up and went to stand behind the boy's chair, her hands holding the back of the chair but not touching him as she bent forward to kiss him on each cheek close to the ear, enveloping him in the scent of her unfamiliar flowers.

The boy would have liked to dance with his mother, round and round in this courtyard with lime-green walls, watched by the little girl with the kitten in her arms, round and round, one two three, one two three, back across the ocean, back to Praslin, back into a time before this present time. But instead he sat very still and then she was gone, walking away on the arm of Uncle Julius and disappearing out of sight.

It was more than three hours later when Evalina and his uncle returned, and they both seemed very tired. They had a young servant with them who carried the bags out into the street and was obedient to any orders. Uncle Julius called him 'my mulatto'. 'Come here, my mulatto! Hurry up, my mulatto!' and the boy presumed that this was his name. It was only later that he understood it was a description of the mixing of black and white skins and that the mulatto was his uncle's child as well as being his uncle's servant.

Outside the hotel a painted cart was waiting, drawn by a team of four big oxen with blue-black lips, their heads heavy from the weight of their horns. In the back of the cart the boy could see most of the luggage they had brought with them on the boat, along with all sorts of anonymous sacks and boxes, a box filled with nervous chickens, a little palm tree with its roots tied up in a cloth bundle and a crate that contained a pig whose pink body was just visible through the wooden slats. The Indian driver sat impassively in the sunshine with a thin whip in his hand and there seemed to be just enough room for one or two people to sit next to him. In the cart itself there was a padded bench facing backwards with a striped canvas awning to provide shade.

The boy wanted to sit next to Evalina in the back, but when she climbed up and settled herself among the cushions she didn't ask him to join her. She had tied a lace scarf around her head in the manner of the Creole women and she looked very severe.

'You sit next to me,' said Uncle Julius, 'then you can tell me about yourself.'

And so he was sandwiched between his uncle smelling of overripe plums and the mulatto smelling of nothing at all. The driver cracked his whip and they set off along streets that were at first familiar but soon became strange. The boy recognised the same beggar who had bowed to them so graciously a few days before, but this time the man was busy sorting through a pile of rubbish that had been left outside a wooden house overgrown with red flowers and creeping green tendrils. The boy looked back as they passed and saw the beggar waving to him as if this was the parting of old friends. He would have liked to wave back but he didn't.

In the dazzling heat the high mountains encircling the town of Port Louis were cut-out silhouettes without any depth or colour.

'They look like men in dark cloaks,' said the boy, thinking of a story he had once been told in which the mountains came alive and strode down into the flat lands searching for food and battle.

'What an extraordinary thing to say,' said his uncle after a pause. 'I have never heard anything so ridiculous. I very much hope that your imagination is not as wild as your mother's, although I suppose it might be. It would be more useful, my boy, to notice that we are now in a sugar plantation. It belongs to me; everything from here to the waterfall at Chamarel belongs to me. Some cane grows to the height of twenty feet or more, but this crop is shorter and of a better quality. "Honey from reeds" Pliny the Elder called it as you shall find out once you have learnt your Latin. I believe the Ancients used bulls' blood to remove the impurities, but now we have lime and cold water which is much more civilised, don't you think?'

'Yes,' said the boy when the silence seemed to demand something from him.

The sugar cane was all around him now. A sea of spears, the white plumes of the flowers glinting in the sunlight. It grew so close together that nobody, not even a small child, could break through such a barrier and escape to the other side. The cart rattled along over a rough dirt road and they went deeper and deeper into the cane that enclosed them for miles around.

They reached a clearing where black men and women were cutting the cane with shining machete blades. The men were naked apart from a cloth tied around their waists and the women were almost naked

as well. Some of the women had babies strapped across
their backs and there was one who had a baby drinking
from her breast as she bent and slashed with her
machete. There were groups of young children sitting
in the sun and dogs milling aimlessly about. The cane
looked so heavy and unyielding and no matter how
much was cut to the ground there was always more of
it, sharp and well defended.

'Have you ever tasted sugar cane?' said Uncle Julius
and the boy shook his head.

'*Disik*, they call it here, but I have no idea where the
word comes from. "*Mo disik*, my mulatto!" and at the
word of command the mulatto sprang down from
the slowly moving cart and snatched a piece of cane
lying on the ground. In a moment he was back in the
cart with the cane across his bare thigh and he was
hacking at it with a little knife. The boy watched him
while he was busy with this task. He had a beautiful
face and his skin and hair gleamed like polished metal.
But now the cane had been divided into two pieces and
without a word the mulatto handed one piece to the
boy and kept the other for himself, chewing at it
thoughtfully with his eyes closed and spitting out the
fibres over the side of the cart.

The boy tasted the cane. Once when he was living
on Praslin a young girl had challenged him to drink
her saliva. Their lips met and she fed him with a warm

sweet water that was more intimate than anything he had ever experienced. The cane brought back that memory as it flooded into his mouth.

Uncle Julius had apparently decided to forget how awkward their attempts at conversation had already been. 'How's your father?' he asked abruptly.

The boy lowered the cane on to his lap and used his tongue to move the sharp fibres out of his mouth and into his clenched fist. This was a difficult question. He had never really known how his father was, except in trying to anticipate and avoid a sudden burst of his anger. 'I am not quite sure,' he said, and then in a rush of confusion he added, 'he has been stamping out copulation, you know, and that has gone quite well I think, although it must be difficult to stamp it out for ever. I was with him in the Valley of May when he shot a man with a pig's face and I think it must have been Bonhomme Michel he shot because he came to our house the next day with his arm in a sling. It was then that my mother became so ill.'

Uncle Julius coughed nervously and looked away. The boy followed his gaze and saw black figures drifting across the landscape with bundles on their heads; he saw piles of big black boulders as high as houses that must have been carefully heaped up by these same men and women, or by their parents or their grand-parents. Two red-legged partridges ran out in front of the cart and zig-zagged across the open fields towards the safety of the cane. In the distance a thick column of smoke ascended towards the sky and he could just see the red flicker of flames at its heart.

# Eighteen

They continued on their way. They left the cane fields and entered a great forest. The track followed the direction of a river with the land rising steeply on either side. The oxen trod cautiously over the rough ground; the cart lurched and shook as it was pulled forward, its wheels rumbling like approaching thunder. There were no people anywhere and no signs of human habitation. The dazzling sunlight of the cleared land had been replaced by a shadowy vegetable light and sometimes the track was enclosed by a roof of leaves so that it was like passing through a tunnel. In the Valley of May you could always walk or run if you wanted to, but here it was different; the trees rose out of a tangle of dense bushes and creepers and you would have to fight for a path through them. The boy remembered what Evalina had told him about the zombies and it was true that many of these trees did look like naked bodies: the bark creased into a fold of smooth skin, softly dented into a navel, swollen into a breast.

There were clumps of wild bananas growing close to the river bank and another palm the boy had never seen before with its leaves spread out in a huge tasselled fan. Suddenly a pink pigeon launched itself from the topmost branch of one of these palms and flew out in front of them with a heavy dipping movement as if it might at any moment sink to the ground with its own weight. It made a wonderful purring sound as it flew past him, so close he could have almost grabbed it from the air. And then it was gone and he was still staring at the empty density of the trees from which it had emerged when there was a series of fierce screeches and yells and a troupe of little monkeys burst out from the undergrowth and were fighting and chasing each other on the track ahead. One of the monkeys had a round fruit in its mouth which gave it a look of bewildered surprise and the others were intent on stealing the fruit. They all had the softly creased faces of old men and old women and the boy could see the sharpness of their teeth when they opened their mouths. He was thinking of what Evalina had said about the monkeys that sometimes climbed on to the veranda of the house somewhere in this forest and he wondered if it was possible to tame them, slowly and with patience.

But now the cart had stopped moving. The boy

was aware that his uncle was lifting a gun and taking aim and he saw the monkey with the fruit in its mouth looking up in the moment when it was already too late. He saw the monkey somersaulting into death; he saw the white tropic birds of Praslin falling like snow out of the sky; the broken snake on the tree; the man escaping over a wooden fence with blood seeping from a wound on his arm. And at a little distance from all this he saw himself kneeling in the sand, challenging the darkness to give him a sign, something that would make all this pain and confusion lie down quietly within his head; something to stop it from clamouring and clawing and drumming at the inside of his skull. He screamed, just as he had screamed before when Bonhomme Michel was shot, and he felt the sound of his own voice thickening around him as if it was trying to protect him from harm.

Somebody, it was not his uncle so it must have been the mulatto, grabbed hold of him and held him tight, but still he continued to be surrounded by the scream that poured out of him. He felt himself being lifted to the ground and carried to the back of the cart where a space had been made for him to lie down with a cushion for his head. People were talking and hovering close but he did not want to look at them so he rolled on to his side and pressed his face against the wooden slats of the crate.

When he was left alone his breathing began to steady itself. The pig in the crate was looking at him with an expression of mild curiosity and he noticed that its pale eyes were flecked with gold, like glittering specks of dust floating in a pool of water; the eyelashes were almost orange. Very gently he inserted his hand between the slats of wood and let his fingers rest against the tight warm skin. Then he went to sleep.

# Nineteen

When the boy woke, the room that he was in seemed familiar to him even though he knew he had never seen it before. The pattern of each day was familiar as well, even though he had no idea when that pattern had first been established.

He got up as soon as it was light, dressed himself, took some food that had been left out for him and went into the garden. He followed a path that led away from the house and there, deep among the trees and noisy with the cascading of the waterfall, he came to the wooden pen and the hut in which the pig lived. The pig belonged to him now. He never paused to wonder who had decided to give it to him, he only knew that it was his and, in some way that he did not need to understand, it protected him from harm.

He came with a basket filled with food: a bunch of the sweet bananas that grew in such profusion close to the stream, scraps from the kitchen, handfuls of green leaves that looked as though they must be good to eat and anything else he could find. He would stop to fill an enamel jug with fresh clear water and then he would clamber over the wooden fence that enclosed the pig's territory and knock politely on the door of the shed in which it slept at night. The pig always answered his greeting with a startled but welcoming grunt and with that signal he walked in, leaving the door wide open so that the mottled sunlight could cover the walls and the floor. He sat on an upturned bucket and presented his offerings to the pig, one by one until they were all gone. Then he filled the trough with water and waited patiently for the hours to begin to pass.

The pig got on with the business of being alive and the boy was content to watch it. Sometimes it would peer at him with a casual curiosity from behind the blinkering of its big pink ears. Sometimes it would come and stand close to him, leaning its heavy body against the side of his knee, and then if he scratched the warm skin where the front legs joined with the chest, it would enter a sort of trance, the tail limp with pleasure, the body swaying as if blown by a wind, the mouth slightly open, the eyes flickering through the orange lashes.

Birds flew across the sky or settled in the trees overhead. There was often the noise of monkeys but they never emerged from the safety of the undergrowth. A few chickens had the habit of entering the pen around midday and they would scratch and search for food before moving on. In the distance the boy might hear people talking, laughing, shouting, singing, but no one came close. As he sat there day after day, he felt he knew exactly what it must be like to be a tree, with roots splayed out in the cold earth, a thin-skinned trunk, branches and leaves and fruit and nothing that needed to be done except to hold on, to feel the warmth of the sunshine, the ripple of wind, the evaporation of dew, the movement of insects. It was a quietness he had never known before.

His food was always left out for him in the kitchen, and one morning, next to the bread and the papaya, the slice of meat and the hard-boiled egg, someone had placed a big tin of white paint, a paintbrush, two planks of wood, a hammer and nails. And so, the boy began to decorate the pig's house.

The walls inside the hut were thick with an accumulation of dust and dirt but he painted straight on top of it, over the trailing spider webs and the yellow nests in which they kept their young, over the layers of dried mud, the cracks in the wood, the place where long ago a rat had started to gnaw a hole. The pig was not particularly interested in all this activity, although it did manage to tread on the paintbrush, leaving a single-footed trail across the concrete floor.

When the walls and the ceiling were gleaming

white, the boy moved out into the enclosed area of the pen and painted the inside of the wooden fencing as well. The work took several days to complete and he was pleased with the result. He then made himself two shelves, one above the other and high enough to be out of reach of the pig's questing nose. On the lower shelf he placed his own supply of food and on the top shelf he set out the treasures he had brought with him from Praslin: the crucifix, the feather from a tropic bird, the land crab's claw, the piece of coral, the snail shell, the pot of musty powder. He even brought out the coco-de-mer and polished it, admiring its gleaming skin. He could spend hours carefully arranging and re-arranging the display, moving things around until he had achieved the desired effect.

At night when the boy returned to the house he would go straight to his room. If he happened to walk past someone then he would quickly look away and it felt as if he was invisible. He was not lonely and for the moment there was nothing that he needed. His room had shuttered windows that cut the sunlight and the moonlight into thin slices. It had a little bed that was decked out like a wedding dress with a fountain of white mosquito netting falling from a hook fixed to the ceiling and bubbling down to the floor. At night when he couldn't sleep he would open the window and if he leaned out he could just see the shed where the pig was sleeping. Sometimes he would sing very softly under his breath, remembering all the songs his mother used to sing to him: the one about the girl who is to be married in the morning with the chorus of words that had no meaning, the one about the woman who was weeping by a river bank, and other songs, many of them.

# Twenty

The boy is lying on his bed with the window open and the first light of dawn is pushing its way among the trees. He is playing with thought. When he closes his eyes it is as if he is floating on his back on a calm sea, the gentle murmuring of water in his ears, the sun warm on his face, the ripples of the pale sand glimmering beneath him.

It is as if the house in which he was born is watching him through its open windows. He can walk into that house when he wants to, entering the room in which his family sits straight-backed around a plain table; a portrait of Jesus as The Light of the World on the wall, a metal crucifix, a barometer, an oil lamp. He goes through a thin door and he is in the room in which his parents sleep, a double and a single bed side by side, both covered with a white counterpane, and he can hear the strange animal sounds that used to confuse him so much, his mind struggling to imagine what was happening.

Now he is in his own room with rustling movements in the roof and the fruit of the coco-de-mer palm wrapped in a cloth and hidden in a cupboard among his clothes because he did not want his mother or his father to know that he had it. That he kept it. That he sometimes placed it on the pillow beside him, his lips close to the shining black skin.

Outside, across the yard and into the dark kitchen where Evalina is plucking a chicken, the feathers falling around her like snow. 'This is what snow is like!' she says. 'Look, the snow is falling in England!' and she throws handfuls of feathers up in the air and watches them drift to the floor.

The snails in the saucepan are stretching out their long necks into the boiling water and for a moment the boy can smell the sharpness of camphor stinging at his nostrils, but with a quick reflex he removes the house and all it contains simply by opening his eyes and staring at the ceiling above him. It is a solid construction with white-painted beams running across it and in the corner close to the window he can see the little gecko which often clings there upside down and pretends to be nothing more than a shadow. Once he tried to feed it with a moth that fluttered enticingly from the captivity of his fingers, but the gecko was much too shy to approach and so he left the moth on the windowsill and perhaps it flew away.

The boy gets up from his bed. He dresses himself.

He opens the door. He has decided to explore the house. The first room he enters is the kitchen. The earth floor is hard and cold under his bare feet. There is the sweet scent of wood ash and spices mixing together. There are bundles of dried herbs hanging from hooks: rosemary he recognises, his mother had rosemary growing in a pot by the door and almost every time he passed he would break off a tip of grey leaves and rub the oily perfume into his fingers. This kitchen is just as dark as the kitchen in the house on Praslin. The eggs in a bowl gleam softly as if suffused with moonlight. Next to them is a bowl of mangoes and he bends over it to breathe in their rich musty smell. A white cloth covers something in a dish but he doesn't lift the cloth because he senses it might hide a dead bird, plucked of its feathers. There is a big water-melon and a knife and a few of those strange fruits that are called *coeurs du boeuf*, bulls' hearts, heart-shaped but pale-skinned as if there was no blood in them and the skin as rough as a cat's tongue. And then a cat does appear and rubs its back against his bare legs. He bends down to stroke it, half expecting it to turn savage and bite him, but it purrs contentedly.

Into the courtyard where he pauses by a big barrel of rainwater, dipping his hand through the glassy sur-face and disturbing a mass of mosquito larvae which shiver so quickly out of sight that it seems as though they were never there. A cockerel crows and another one answers it from far away.

He opens a heavy door and walks along a corridor. He looks into each room as he passes: a store-room filled with wooden barrels, a room in which there are three huge bunches of green bananas and some sacks that must be filled with sugar, an empty room, a baking room with a big oven, a washroom with bundles of sheets on the floor.

Another door leads him into a grand hallway. The walls are lined with wooden panelling, there are carpets on the floor and beautifully carved banisters follow the sweeping line of a staircase. He climbs the stairs step by step, but each one seems to be set at a different angle so that it is like walking on a ship's deck with the sea lurching beneath and he has to steady himself by holding tightly to the banisters. There is a painting of a stern-looking man on the wall: a gold chain around his neck, a monkey on his shoulder, a book on the table in front of him. The boy thinks this might be a portrait of one of his relatives.

From the window at the top of the stairs there is a view out across the forest: an ocean of green. The dawn is growing brighter although the light is still dim and quiet. It is just possible to see the waterfall tipping endlessly over the edge of a cliff and down into a pool below. When he is with the pig the boy can hear the waterfall pattering like his own heartbeat, but here it makes no sound.

Now he is standing in front of a door and from behind it there comes a rasping, growling sound as if there was a fierce beast trapped in the room and desperate to escape. The boy opens the door very very carefully. The room is dominated by a four-poster bed and his Uncle Julius is lying on it on his back, the sheets tangled around him, his legs sprawled and his swollen penis twitching and moving on his belly like the sea slugs on the floor of the ocean. His mouth is wide open which is probably why he is snoring so loudly and the curtains are blowing through the open windows just as they did in the house on Praslin.

It is only after a few moments that the boy notices the naked woman who is lying beside his uncle, her body folded so closely against his that she seems like his shadow. She turns in her sleep and moves her thigh to cover his nakedness. She turns again and lifts her head from the pillow, staring towards the boy from behind the dark tangle of her hair, but he already has his back to her and then the door closes softly behind him.

There are other rooms. A room with nothing in it but a full-length mirror and a line of clothes hanging from a railing. A room with an empty bed that looks as though it has been recently slept in. A room that is locked. The boy is about to go down the stairs when he hears a door handle turning and two figures emerge on to the landing. One of them reminds him of Evalina and the other one reminds him of his mother when he saw her standing naked in front of him, but that was such a long time ago. They walk past quite close to where he is standing but they do not notice him.

Down the stairs and into a library with leather-bound volumes on the shelves that reach as high as the ceiling, and glass doors that are standing wide open. The boy runs out into the garden, over a lawn of rough grass that feels like wire under his bare feet, past a tree with huge dangling leaves, around a corner, along a path and finally he is back in familiar territory. There is the tree with the ripening bulls' hearts hidden among its leaves and he can already hear the distant rush of the waterfall.

He stands in the shallow stream to pick a bunch of watercress. He finds a ripe mango that must have been dropped by someone because there are no mango trees growing in this part of the garden. He is on his way to the pig. When he gets to the hut he sees that a long rope has been left next to the fence, neatly coiled so that it looks like a sleeping snake. He thinks he could make a collar and a lead for the pig with it. Why not? Then they could go walking together. They could go exploring.

# Twenty-one

If someone had been watching from the house quite early on the next morning they would have seen the boy and the pig setting off. They pause to drink from the stream before wading through the shallow water side by side. Then they are threading their way along a narrow path until they reach the place where the women come to wash clothes: rubbing them on the big flat rocks, rinsing them in a clear pool and stretching them out to dry on the bushes, the cloth stiffening in the sun.

Now the boy and the pig turn away from the stream and disappear among the trees. Their path here is overgrown with guava bushes that cover the ground with a tangle of thin branches making it difficult to walk, but they seem to be sure of the direction they are taking and do not often hesitate.

The pig leads and the boy follows. Soon they are surrounded by the enormous ancient trees that once covered most of the island before there was sugar cane and houses. The sunlight trickles through the leaves like thin columns of water and you almost expect to feel it wet and cold against your skin. The bark of the trees glistens where a patch of sunlight touches it and then it seems to pulsate with life as if it contained a beating heart. The boy looks up at the pale ferns that hang in bundles from the branches and he suddenly remembers what they are called. 'They are called cows' tongues and bulls' tongues,' he says, laughing because the names are so unsuitable, because cows and bulls have thick moist tongues that are almost black, while these ferns are such a delicate luminous green.

They continue on their way until they reach a little clearing among the trees. Here there is a low flowering bush that is similar to one the boy has seen growing in his uncle's garden, and a wooden hut, its roof thatched with bundles of dried grass.

'Let's stop here,' says the boy and he sits himself down among the spreading roots of a tree at the edge of the clearing. A cluster of tiny birds suddenly bursts out of the bush and flies excitedly into the air. 'Maybe they are zozos,' says the boy, pulling a white handkerchief from his pocket and waving it around. In a moment several of the birds are fluttering close to him and one of them brushes the tip of its wing feathers against his cheek while another lands on his head so that he can feel the delicate pricking of its feet through his hair. 'Look! Look at the zozos!' he says, but the sound of his voice frightens them and they fly away.

The pig is lying quietly on its side in the shade of the tree and it doesn't stir when the boy stretches out his foot and runs his toes along the length of its back. Now that the zozo birds have gone he is shocked by the silence all around him and the lack of movement. Ferns hang, branches reach, leaves are suspended; everything seems to be holding its breath and waiting.

The boy is also waiting, caught up in the stillness. He stares into the dark curtain of the trees until he can see something moving there; a pale bird is walking towards him with awkward halting steps. It emerges into the bright sunlight, its legs a waxy yellow and its feathers white apart from a tuft of black near the base of the tail, but it's the head with the huge beak that startles the boy, the eyes blank and the beak such a terrible heavy claw. The dodo moves nearer until it is standing directly in front of him. It is so close that he could grab hold of it if he wanted to. Then it walks away, slow and ponderous, and is soon lost within the surrounding darkness.

The boy becomes aware of a stirring noise as if the wind was rattling at the shutters of his bedroom window. Again he looks into the curtain of darkness and this time he can just distinguish a crowd of tortoises huddled together among the trees, male and female, young and old, there must be at least a hundred of them. The largest makes its way forward into the centre of the clearing and the boy recognises its sweet and gentle face at once. It stands very still and waves its extended neck from side to side, the weight of the huge shell held high above the ground on stiffened legs. Then with a strange hissing sigh it sinks down and begins to tear at the grass, the pink tongue moving between toothless gums. The other tortoises are reassured that there is no danger and soon the clearing is covered by a blanket of shells, muttering and clicking, bone to bone.

A cool breeze springs up out of nowhere, causing the leaves on the trees to shake and whisper. Some of the tortoises close their eyes and stretch out their necks with pleasure, rocking from side to side in a subdued ecstasy. The boy closes his eyes as well, the air caressing his face like the tips of fingers. For a moment he seems to be lost in sleep and when he again looks around all the tortoises have gone and the pig is standing very close to him, the heat of its body against his leg.

'Don't be afraid,' says the pig in a funny muffled voice as if its mouth were full of pebbles.

A man has just come out of the hut. He is rubbing his glistening body with oil and as he does so his skin begins to crease and fold and slip away under the pressure of his hand until it has fallen from him and lies on the ground in a heap like an old coat. Then the boy sees black hair erupting along the man's legs and arms and across his belly. He sees him taking on a new face that is savage and incomprehensible. A woman is standing beside him now and she is also shuffling out of her skin, but she emerges from it as soft and pale as something that has been living under a stone and her transparent body is throbbing with its own heartbeat. The two figures turn and walk towards the boy, their arms outstretched to clasp him.

'Quick,' says the pig. 'Climb on my back!' The boy does as he is told, gripping the tight skin of the neck with both hands and lying forward so that he will not fall. They race through the forest, over the stream and back into the house. The boy cannot remember if he walked the last few steps to his bedroom or if the pig carried him. That night he had many dreams, noisy dreams filled with a clamour of voices.

# Twenty-two

There is a knocking at the door of the bed-room which startles the boy since no one has attempted to make any contact with him since he first came to this house. And how long ago is that? He has no idea.

He opens the door and there is the mulatto. He is wearing a white shirt and his black hair has been care-fully sculpted with a parting on one side and the curls smoothed away. The boy is startled to see how closely this face resembles his own.

The mulatto stands there very tight and formal. 'Uncle Julius would like to know if you are ready to begin your lessons,' he says. 'I have brought you some clothes which should fit, and shoes, very nice shoes but no socks yet, we hope to get them tomorrow. Your teacher is an Englishman called Mr Swann. I expect he'll teach you everything you need to know and that will be an end to it. Mr Swann and your uncle would like to see you in half an hour. I'll come to collect you.'

There is a great deal that the boy would like to say during the few minutes of this encounter, but he says nothing, only smiling as he takes the clothes and nodding his head foolishly. When the mulatto has gone he turns to face the room which has been crowded with all the things of his imagination but which now looks so empty and lifeless.

The clothes fit him perfectly. It feels odd to have his legs covered in long trousers and his feet are uncomfortable within the hard shoes, but maybe the socks will remove that problem. His father used to wear shoes even when he went walking along the shining beach at Praslin, leaving a trail of heavy solid steps stretching out behind him in the sand. The boy remembers the sound of his father's footsteps as he walked through the house. His mother preferred not to wear shoes except on Sundays and when she entered the church. She had long toes.

The mulatto returns and together they set off towards the library. There are people everywhere; the boy has never seen so much activity, or maybe he has never noticed it before. Three young girls in the kitchen start to laugh as he approaches and they make him feel ashamed although he doesn't know what he is ashamed of. Doors open and close. He bumps into a woman carrying a basin filled with water and she shouts at him angrily.

They walk across the slippery floor of the entrance hall, the mulatto silent on bare feet, the boy clattering just as his father had clattered. They enter the library with its view out on to the veranda and there is Uncle Julius sitting behind a shining table and a little man with hunched shoulders sitting next to him. The little man makes Uncle Julius look even bigger and heavier than he is, and when he rises to his feet and strides towards the boy it is as if a genie has escaped from its bottle and is towering in the air above him. There is something which might be the fruit bat hanging on the back of his uncle's chair, but it doesn't move or unwrap its leathery wings.

'That's right, here we are,' says Uncle Julius, gripping the boy's shoulders. 'Good, good, good,' he says and he shakes him so that the boy is reminded of his mother being shaken long ago. 'I hear that you have settled in? Got to know your way around, yes? And now you are ready for a little learning and Mr Swann here will be your guide, won't you, Mr Swann?'

The moment he heard his name being mentioned Mr Swann had stood up and stepped forward, but now he hovers in uncertainty, waiting for some further instruction. The skin of his face is stretched tightly over the bones and it has a strange greyness to it. He doesn't look at all well, his body trembles and there is a glistening film of sweat above his upper lip. 'Touch of malaria,' he says by way of justification and he wipes his face with his sleeve. 'Been out too long in the sun, but I manage. And what do they call you, boy?'

The boy is overwhelmed by confusion. He has never been called anything; he has been a child, a petit dodo when he couldn't sleep, a fool when he didn't listen, but he had never been a name except when he wrote it on a piece of paper or on the flyleaf of a book. 'Eliel,' he replies, embarrassed by the sound the word makes and the foreignness of it as it reverberates through his head.

'Eliel?' says Mr Swann, raising his dusty eyebrows so that his wide brow is suddenly alive with rippling lines. 'Eliel? Eliel? Don't know it! Must be biblical I suppose, but I haven't come across it. Belial of course we do know, don't we?'

'Belial?' repeats the boy in a helpless echo.

'Never heard of Belial? Shame on you! He first appears in the Old Testament where he signifies emptiness, worthlessness, but then he slowly takes shape as it were, until he has turned into the name for the devil himself. El is the Hebrew Jehovah and Bel is his other half, the dark creature of the pit.'

'Fascinating,' interrupts Uncle Julius, rubbing his hands together so that they rustle like snakes. 'Well, I must leave you to your studies, my dear Eliel. Get a good grasp of ancient history and the scriptures and

I'm sure you'll have all you need. Personally I've always found a knowledge of the weather useful. It pays to know when a storm is on its way. But I must be off. Hurry up, my mulatto, we have work to do.' And out they go, the door swinging shut behind them.

'Sit down, Eliel,' says Mr Swann, motioning to the second chair which he has moved so that it faces him across the table. If there was a fruit bat, it isn't there now. 'Sit down and let me look at you', and he runs the back of his hand across his lip, pausing while another tremor passes through his thin body.

The boy sits, silent and obedient. He feels the sweat trickling down his back, like tears he thinks but he tries to dismiss the thought. He begins to count the rings on the shining wood of the table, to see how old the tree was when it was cut down.

'Your uncle believes that your future lies in the Church,' says Mr Swann. 'My job is to get you ready for England so that you can complete your studies there. Your uncle is confident that in England you can pass as a white man with a dark skin, while here you will always be a mulatto, a Creole, a child of the island as they sometimes call it. I understand that it was an unfortunate marriage between your poor mother and your father; the two races should never be mixed. You might like to read this little book that your uncle has just given to me. It names all the local families who are black even though they would like to be thought of as white. Your mother's maiden name is there, of course, but your father's family is not included. I'm sure you can understand the problem.'

The boy picks up the book that is held out to him. He knows that within this moment his childhood has come to an end and now nothing will ever be the same again because the threads of his first life have been broken. The spider threads that cling to his face and hands, he can wipe them away and rub them between his finger and thumb like fragments of old skin. He can forget everything.

# Part III

# Twenty-three

U p the stairs, along a corridor, faster and faster, feet on a hard floor, heart pattering like a mouse on its exercise wheel, faster and faster.

Up more stairs and along another corridor. I turn my head to see the reflection of my own face in the dark glass of a window and for a moment I wonder who that person might be, man or woman, young or old; but then the window has gone and I am surrounded once more by the bare monotony of white walls. I gaze down at the floor which is grey with a dim shine to it as if it were covered by a thin film of water. The soles of my shoes make a soft clicking sound with each step that I take.

I come to an open door and stop to look inside. There is my grandfather as a child of about twelve years old and the book is still in his hand. He doesn't notice me, but Mr Swann swings round to face me and his eyes are as sharp as swords. I suddenly realise that he is very similar in appearance to the shaking man who was buried up to his neck in the sands of the desert long ago; perhaps the two are really the same but I never noticed the connection before.

There is a dazzle of light from the long windows on the far side of the room but I cannot tell if beyond them is a tropical forest and the singing of unfamiliar birds, or a cold garden with rose petals scattered on the wet grass of the lawn. I look again at the child's face, hoping that he will turn to me, but his concentration cannot be broken and so I leave as quietly as possible.

I am back in the corridor and almost running now. I wonder why I am so afraid. I can feel the fear tingling at the ends of my fingers, pressing against my eyes, tumbling down within the cavity of my body. I long to finish the telling of this story because only then will I be able to step away from the fear, shuffle it off like a skin that has grown too tight.

I have entered a room that has five empty beds in it, three along one wall and two along the other. Each bed is made up so tightly that it looks as though no one could ever pull them open; perhaps you would need to cut through the sheets with a knife. The sixth bed is occupied and a woman is lying in it wrapped up in a sheet so that only her face is exposed. I know her at once. This must be the boy's mother, but she has grown so old. I wonder how long she has been here.

Her head is arched back, her eyes and mouth are wide open, her breathing is slow and laboured. I don't think she can move or speak but I feel ashamed of seeing her like this; it is a terrible intrusion on her privacy even if she is not directly aware of my presence.

I mumble an apology and as I walk away I am suddenly reminded of the time when I visited my father in a hospital room that was similar to this one. He was all on his own with empty well-made beds on either side of him. He was lying with his face pressed into the pillow and when he turned towards the sound of my voice he was more unfamiliar to me than someone I had never seen in my life before. He had black rings around his eyes that looked as though they had been painted on with theatrical greasepaint and his face was a soft clay that had been pulled and tugged so that the features were lost and distorted. 'Oh God I am so unhappy,' he said, and then he started to laugh until his eyes were bright with tears.

There is a rumbling sound and I look up to see a figure in a white uniform moving towards me along the corridor, pushing something that could be a trolley or a bed and it is the turning wheels that are making the noise. The figure glimmers in the distance like a mirage and almost imperceptibly it moves closer until it has stopped just in front of me. I see a woman with dark skin and big flat teeth; she could be Evalina

Larose but I am not sure. It is a bed that she has been pushing and there is a person on the bed who is completely concealed by a white sheet.

I suddenly remember what I am looking for. 'Excuse me,' I say, 'I am trying to find the geriatric ward. Could you tell me where it is?'

I am told to go up some more stairs and along another corridor until I come to wide doors that open as I approach as if they had been expecting me. The air smells of peppermints and camphor and something rather musty. I have come here to talk to the old man my grandfather.

# Twenty-four

I am in a big room with the light coming in through big windows. There are no beds here but an assortment of armchairs, some on their own, some clustered together in groups, some empty, some occupied. A semi-circle of armchairs is gathered around the television that sits under one of the windows. The sunlight drains most of the colour from the screen but it is still possible to see the image of horses with long necks galloping over green grass, the men on their backs clinging to them like insects. It reminds me of the story of the boy riding on the pig in the forest of his childhood, although I suppose it would never really be possible to do that, you would quickly slip from the smooth hot body, lying there helpless among the damp leaves with the pig gone home long ago. My father told me that he once tried to ride a pig; he jumped on and grabbed hold of the ears but the pig tore him loose by dragging him against a barbed-wire fence.

There is a babble of sound all around me. The commentator's voice rising and falling in muted excitement, the chink of a china teacup on a saucer, the scrape of a chair being moved, a muttered string of words. I look at a sea of old men and old women. How many are there, twenty perhaps? I remind myself that I have come to talk to my grandfather who must be here somewhere. Anyway I can still smell the camphor and peppermints and that peculiar mustiness of his so I could surely find him even if I was blindfolded.

In the first corner of the room, a dark corner that seems to have escaped from the reach of the sunlight, there sits the oldest and smallest woman I have ever seen. She is crumpled into her enormous chair like a shrivelled foetus, one hand lost in the sleeve of her cardigan, the other hand lying discarded on her lap as if someone had found it on the floor and placed it there for safety. She is talking to herself softly and intensely, hardly pausing to take breath. 'And after that,' she says, 'after that I was going. This place is not fit for anyone, I said. After that I said, I'm going. I'm going, I said to them. After that I said goodbye, I'm going. And after that this is still the place I shan't be in. And then The Fight. And after that, at this time, *now*, I am going. This is not the place for anyone to be in, I said.'

Next to her is a woman who sleeps with her mouth wide open and empty of teeth and then a woman who stares fixedly at the wall and seems to be on the edge of tears and a man who plays dominoes by himself at a little table, picking up the black pieces and sucking them between soft lips before putting them down with a snap. He builds an interconnecting network of numbers and then swishes them round into a confusion and begins again.

And there is my grandfather in his chair, his hands folded together on his lap twitching and fluttering as if they were dreaming their own dreams, separate from the rest of the body. Having followed him in my thoughts as a child I can still see the child in his face, or at least I tell myself that I can. The gold ring has gone from his finger and the dog-collar has been removed from around his neck. The dome of his head is polished and shining and the little scattering of white hair looks as soft as eiderdown. His skin is yellow and reptilian and once again I am reminded of a tortoise and remember that I dreamt of a tortoise only a few days ago: it was lying huge and abandoned in a shed and in the dream I was very shocked because I hadn't realised it had always been there.

My grandfather's bottom lip is trembling, the pink tongue protrudes for a moment and then withdraws. His eyes are almost closed but I think he might be watching me.

By way of a greeting I gently take one of his cold

hands and it comes to life and grips me with a sudden fierceness. 'You are quite right,' he says. 'Mr Swann was the end of my childhood. Everything changed after that and I grew up and came here. But there was the storm on the day after I met Mr Swann and that was an odd coincidence, don't you think?'

'The storm,' I say, 'tell me about the storm.'

My grandfather pauses, his head tipped forward to his chest, his hand still holding mine. 'I rather enjoyed it,' he says softly. 'April 29th, 1892 and it began with the first light of dawn and went on until eight in the evening although it was dark through much of the day, as dark as night with all that rain. I was woken by the noise of the wind and then the mulatto—you know him, don't you—he came to tell me to come quickly to the library. Everyone was busy bolting the doors and the shutters and outside you could hear the shouts and cries of animals and people, but I don't know what happened to them, there was nowhere else as safe as the library. The wind raced faster and faster, the trees cracking and splitting and roof tiles and broken branches and anything else that couldn't hold rushing through the air. All the summer benches on the veranda were lifted up and thrown into the stream near where the women used to go to wash the clothes. The rain was so heavy it poured down the walls of the library like a waterfall, over the paintings and over the books in the bookcase, and then it crept out across the floor and around the legs of the table and the chairs and all we could do was watch.

'Then,' and my grandfather heaves himself into an upright position, his old eyes very wide, staring into the distance, 'then the roaring stopped and the hissing of the rain stopped and everything went hushed because we were in the eye of the storm. I looked out through the slats in the shutters and the garden was covered in a blanket of hazy mist just like an English mist coming in from the meadows although I hadn't seen that yet. It looked so peaceful and quiet and I thought the worst was over until the wind came back twice as strong as before. The whole side of the house where my bedroom and the kitchens were, was demolished in a moment. All the little living quarters and sheds out in the garden were gone as well, swept away and nothing left of them.'

My grandfather lapses back into silence and at first I think that he must have fallen asleep, but as I look at him I realise that he is walking through the streets of Port Louis, inspecting the damage that was inflicted by the storm. He wrinkles his nose at the stench of decay that hangs in the air. He crosses his feet in their felt slippers as he steps carefully over the swollen corpse of a dead dog, over the bales of brightly coloured silk that have burst out of a shop window and now lie derelict in the gutter, over all the rubble and confusion that surrounds him. Down by the market there is a cargo ship that has been swept bodily out of the sea and thrown on to the street, spilling its load of polished rice that is already beginning to ferment in a huge stinking heap. My grandfather goes to the Hotel Universe and is glad to see that it has survived even though it looks very battered. Somebody tells him about the horse that managed to swim to safety through one of the bedroom windows and they found it there in the morning, standing between two beds. He laughs to himself when he thinks of that.

# Twenty-five

Now it is time for tea. The same nurse who had been pushing a bed along one of the corridors appears with a trolley laden with metal urns, jugs of milk and bowls of sugar, cups and saucers and a few plastic beakers with a little spout for those who are no longer able to drink from a cup. There are even two sorts of cake to choose from: jam Swiss roll or chocolate Viennese fingers.

'Cake,' says a thin voice behind me. 'Cake, cake, cakey, cake', but when I turn round I cannot tell who was speaking. I'm not even sure if it was a man or a woman.

'That's Evalina Larose,' whispers my grandfather, raising the index finger of his right hand and pointing in her direction. 'She's the same Evalina Larose I knew when I was a child although she is much blacker now than she used to be. You'll smell her in a minute, she smells of sex, she always did. You watch when she comes with my cake and you'll see how she presses her breasts against me. Sometimes she pretends she wants to wash me and starts tugging at my clothes. That's because she wants to see my testicles, to see if they are as dark as she thinks they are. But I won't let her see them. I fight with her.'

Evalina Larose is busy. She puts a slice of cake wrapped in a paper napkin on the lap of the woman who is telling the story of what happened next during her long life. The hand and the cake lie side by side, motionless. She puts a slice of cake on the table of the man who is playing dominoes and he breaks it up into little bits and looks at it thoughtfully. She gives cake to the woman who is on the verge of tears and some to the woman who was fast asleep but who stirs now, blinking open her eyes that are as blue as a summer sky. She offers cake to everyone who is busy watching the horses on the television and there is a brief flurry of excitement as the choice is made between the jam and the chocolate. Most prefer the chocolate.

My grandfather is getting restless. 'Chocolate,' he says mournfully, 'but there won't be any left unless she hurries up. Oh hurry up, Evalina! Do hurry up!' and his feet scrabble on the floor while his hands tighten on the arm-rests as he tries to make the first effort towards standing.

Finally Evalina Larose bustles forward. She pats my

grandfather on his sharp knees and says, 'What would you like, my dear, the one with the jam or the one with the chocolate?'

'Chocolate,' he replies peevishly and as she brings a tray with its plastic beaker of tea and a piece of cake, he lunges towards her and manages to rub the side of his old head against her breasts. The tray totters but she doesn't drop it. She sets it down carefully on his lap and smiles at him quite sweetly. He looks into her black eyes and remembers all the stories she told him while they were on the boat and how he has been afraid of zombies and the loup-garou ever since. He remembers her singing voice that used to creep across his skin and how he wanted to ask her to stroke him and kiss him and how she went away and he never knew where she had gone. He places a tiny piece of cake in his mouth and waits for her to recognise him, but she is much too busy and before he can say anything she has gone back to her trolley and she is leaving the room, followed by the rumbling of the wheels that sounds like distant thunder.

'She climbs into bed with me when she thinks I'm asleep,' my grandfather says, very matter-of-fact now that she has gone. 'She's like a big snake creeping over me, licking and biting. She wraps me up in her arms and legs and breathes into my neck. If she's too heavy I can always ring the night-bell and then she's gone in a minute. She doesn't want to be found out or she might lose her job. They're all here, you know,' and he sucks noisily at his beaker of tea. 'Mr Swann is here, but I want to avoid him because he was a harsh man. My uncle is here somewhere and so is my father although I haven't seen him for such a long time I can hardly picture his face. My mother is in the room downstairs, but she is not well and nobody is allowed to disturb her. I suppose I could just go and stand next to her bed, she might appreciate that in a way. And I saw your father a few days ago, he walked through this room and close to where I am sitting but he didn't see me and he looked mad, quite mad. He had his arm in a sling and I suppose that was why he made me think of Bonhomme Michel. It might be wise to keep away from him for a while; he could be very dangerous.'

# Twenty-six

The hours go by and it is dark outside. I am in a long room with six old men sleeping in their beds and I am sitting in a straight-backed chair close to the window. The curtains are drawn and the strips of fluorescent lighting have been turned off, but there is a muted glow coming from somewhere, an under-water light in which everything seems to float and distances are hard to judge.

I had never imagined that there would be so much noise. Six old men lie on their backs with their heads propped on big pillows and each one groans and mutters and snores within the private capsule of sleep. One man is whispering to himself as if he was two lovers locked in a secret embrace. Another is muttering curses, a string of words pulled out of him inch by inch, damning the world and everything in it. 'Horrible,' he says. 'What a bloody yawn. Well, fuck it, what a bloody day. Oh the buggers, oh how horrible!' and he lapses into silence before gathering strength for another attack.

The man in the bed nearest to where I am sitting quietly opens one eye and stares at me, a blank expressionless gaze, and then the eye closes and he is gone. I wonder if he will remember me in the morning. Maybe I will have been his mother sitting by his bedside waiting for him to recover from an illness, or his wife thinking about leaving him, or even an angel on Judgement Day, assessing the value of his soul and whether he is fit for heaven or for hell.

I am suddenly aware of someone moving. I look down the line of beds and see that it is the oldest of all the men here, a luminously pale creature with a sharp beak of a nose and heavily lidded eyes. He seems to be made from a combination of bird and reptile, a lizard that is about to stretch its leathery wings and learn how to fly. As slowly as a dancer he lifts one thin branch of an arm up into the air, and there it hangs, the hand drooping and limp, the skin so soft and white it might never have been exposed to the daylight. Then as I watch I see the other hand gently crawling out of the casing of the sheets and creeping up the first, over the shoulder and along the bone to the elbow and the wrist, stroking the skin with a rhythmic sweeping gesture. The two arms remain in the air for a while and then they are slowly lowered to fold quietly across the chest. The man yawns with a huge opening of his mouth and sighs very sweetly like a young girl. This is as close as I have ever been to seeing a ghost: a long languid ghost who might be found haunting a marsh, rising up like steam from a pool of water and then being swept away by the wind, calling out a person's name as he goes.

My grandfather has been sleeping peacefully, but now he stirs. 'Oh no, oh no, oh somebody help me, oh somebody please!' His voice is almost that of a child even though he looks so old. A nurse comes to him with the squeak of her shoes and the rustling of her skirt and she asks him what is the matter and what does he need. He wants to say that he is afraid of lying on his back because of the weight of the darkness pressing down on his face and the sharpness of the bag of stones tied around his waist and digging into his flesh. He is afraid of the man in the next bed whose long arms are like the branches of the *makak* tree and the *bois du pomme*. He wants to say how glad he is that she has come to him and how much he has missed her and how he did visit her before he left the island but maybe she didn't see him. He walked into the room where they kept her and she didn't move or blink or turn her head and there was nothing, nothing, nothing he could do to help her. That was why he left and he is sorry that he had to leave and hopes that she will forgive him.

'There is something in my bed,' he says to the nurse. 'I can't sleep, I'm not comfortable, I think it might be cockroaches.' The nurse pulls back the covers and brushes her hand across the smooth surface of the sheet. 'Biscuits,' she says. 'Biscuits and look here are your pills that would help you to sleep if only you swallowed them when you were supposed to. And what on earth is this? It looks like a broken crab's claw and smells like it too, how disgusting!' and she sweeps the crumbs, the pills and the broken crab's claw into the palm of her hand and tips them into a plastic bin. 'Are you all right now?' she asks. 'Better?'

'No I'm not,' he says, trying with all the energy of his mind to make her see him and take pity. 'I've been bitten by something, my skin hurts. There are dark patches on it like bruises, maybe I am ill', and he begins to struggle with the buttons of his pyjamas, exposing a hairy belly.

But there is another noise from a bed further down the line, an urgent stifled noise, and the nurse has no more time for my grandfather. She folds him quickly back into his sheets and she is gone.

'Cuckoo,' he calls to her softly. 'Cuckoo, I am here. Cuckoo, cuckoo', but she does not return.

I get up from my chair by the window and come to stand beside him, thinking he might be glad to see a familiar face. He looks at me with deep suspicion and says, 'I don't know who you are but you don't belong here. You had better go.' Which I do straight-away, glad to leave the room for a while and to step out into the bright light of the corridor.

# Twenty-seven

The night has moved on and I suppose it must be around two o'clock in the morning. I was away for a while but now I am back in this room of sleeping men. The air all around me is struggling with the effort of breathing; the room itself seems to heave and sigh like some huge stranded fish that has been pulled out of the water.

The man who was swearing so violently has nothing more to say, neither does the whispering one, or the bird-reptile one whose white hands lie folded across his chest in the same position as when I last saw them.

My grandfather is also asleep. I look at his face expecting to see it serene and tranquil but it's not that at all and I realise he is caught up in a net of urgent restless dreams that are flickering through his head. He is dreaming of leaving the island all those years ago and it is a dream that often comes to him at this particular time of the night, the deepest point when there is the most silence.

In his dream my grandfather walks into a room
that is filled with black metal trunks and each one has
his name written on it in white letters. He had three
trunks exactly like these which he took with him when
he left the island and he could remember packing
them and the strange sensation that came from filling
them with everything he possessed. Later, when he and
his wife and his son were living in the vicarage he kept
copies of his sermons in one of these trunks: page after
page of handwritten advice and exhortation to the people of his parish, urging them above all to avoid the sin
of lust and the danger of unnecessary fornication. He
described the devil as a black man who walked through
the streets of their northern village searching for an
evil thought or deed that he could hold on to and use
as a lever. He told them that he had once seen the devil
with his arm in a sling trying to enter the house in
which he lived when he was a child and he looked
more terrible than words could say. And because he
came from a far-away country he was able to tell them
from personal experience how black men smell of fornication and how the women parade themselves like
the Whore of Babylon and so it was easy to see why
intermarriage between the two races was a worse danger to the safety of the world than any number of
atomic bombs.

Anyway, here is my grandfather in his dream in a
room that is crowded with trunks. They remind him of

that gathering of tortoises in the forest, their shells so close he could walk across their backs from one side of the clearing to the other. But now he must not let himself be distracted, he must pack as quickly as he can because the boat will go without him unless he hurries. He opens the first trunk and it is filled with sea slugs, filled to the brim with a moving soup of those creatures and their sweet salty smell. Some of them have been damaged and he can see that under the thin layer of black skin their bodies are as white as snow.

The next trunk contains the fruit of the coco-de-mer, the same one that he brought with him from Praslin and even brought to England, hiding it carefully under a heap of clothes so that no one would know that he had it. But as he looks at the nut it begins to pulsate with life and the shiny black thighs open like a clam under water, revealing the wound of a woman's sex.

He opens the third trunk and there is the mulatto, lying as if in a coffin, very smart in a white suit but with his mouth sewn up so that he cannot answer if a sorcerer calls for him, wishing to turn him into a zombie.

My poor grandfather doesn't know what to do. He shuts the lids of the trunks with a snap and then he runs across their backs, out through the glass doors. He is on a boat now, in a little cabin with two bunk-beds just like the ones in the boat that first took him away

from Praslin. The moon is staring in through the porthole, but the moon has his mother's face, her skin
caked with white powder, and she licks her lips as she
pulls closer and closer to the glass until she is occupy-
ing it entirely. He looks away and a woman he has
never seen before leans out of the bunk above him and
peers down at him with greedy eyes. She climbs hot
and wet into his bed and drinks his seed which he
knows is the greatest sin of all so that he is afraid he
might go mad and be locked away in his madness.
The woman sighs and falls asleep on top of him, her leg
over his thigh, her hair covering his face.

My grandfather is struggling to return to wakefulness. His body jolts and twitches. He opens his eyes and
sees the white skin of the old bird-reptile man in the
next bed and he thinks that this must be his wife. Her
skin has a similar whiteness to it, with a blue tinge like
thin milk, and she is always soft and cold as if her flesh
is a congealed liquid. He wants to clamber into bed with
her now, to rest his hand authoritatively on her white
belly because she belongs to him, to look into her blue
eyes, to touch her red hair, to kiss her closed lips and to
possess her formally and without passion. He remembers the shock when their first child was born and
brought to him screaming like a wild animal with a
mat of soft black feathery hair that covered most of his
forehead and a dark skin that was almost purple. 'He

has your eyes,' said the midwife as she handed over this bundle of steaming rage, and he had wanted to dash the creature's brains out because it had betrayed him.

My grandfather rolls to the side of his bed and his hand grasps the metal rail that is there to protect him from falling. He is comforted by the coldness. He returns to his sleep, his face tranquil now that the dreams have left him.

# Twenty-eight

My grandfather watches the first light of the dawn coming in through a gap in the curtains. He doesn't for a moment doubt that he is lying in his own bed at the vicarage, with the cedar tree in the garden that his wife loves so much and the church on the other side of the hedge. In his mind he follows the path that leads from the garden to the church: across the lawn, under the rose trellis, beside the red-brick wall where the branches of the peach tree are stretched out on wires as if to make them confess some crime, through a little wooden gate and into the graveyard. The gravestones are massive: great slabs of granite leaning against the wind and filled like the pages of a book with so many names. One has ten children on it, all gone before their parents, and there is another on which a boy's Christian name appears three times as if the same person kept on returning to the world but always failed to struggle out of his own childhood.

My grandfather stares vaguely towards the chair next to the window and he sees it as his chair at home, an uncomfortable chair to sit on, but useful for clothes. His empty shoes are side by side underneath it, his shirt and underwear are folded neatly on the seat and his trousers hang over the back with peppermints in one pocket, mothballs and the tin of musty powder in the other. He once put a mothball in his mouth mistaking it for a peppermint; it had a strange soapy consistency and a horrible taste that was hard to get rid of. The saliva rises in his mouth with the memory.

His dog-collar is on the dressing-table next to the soft red wig that his wife puts on each morning, a sleeping cat to keep her head warm; dog and cat, man and wife, side by side. Her hairbrush is there as well, made from ivory and pig bristle which always seems such an odd conjunction of beasts. Everything in this room is so intensely familiar he can see it with his eyes closed: the carpet splashed with flowers, the wardrobe with its long mirror on the inside of the door in which you can never see more than a silhouette of yourself because of the way the light shines. He reaches out his hand to the bedside table and touches the leather cover of the Bible that lies there. He sometimes lets it fall open at random in the hope of finding some interesting reflection on the day, but recently it keeps opening at the picture of Samson being betrayed, his hair lying like snakes on the marble floor and Delilah laughing at him. It must be something to do with the binding; he should have the book repaired.

He can hear the shallow breathing of his wife in the next bed, a restless watery sound. She has a fastidious way of breathing as if she resented the intrusion of air into her lungs. When he first met her she appeared to him as an apparition of Englishness: pale-skinned and smelling of lavender, surrounded on all sides by a crowd of dead and living relations, droves of them scattered in houses and graveyards throughout the region, all with the same hooded red eyelids and icy blue eyes. Only a few members of her family agreed to come to the wedding and one aunt whispered it about that the groom must have a great deal of black blood in him, she could see it at once and hear it in the way that he spoke. Belial they called him, but only in private and amongst themselves.

Never mind. There is a scuffling sound from behind the bed; it might be a rat, they always come back inside the house when the weather gets colder. The other day he saw the tail of a rat hanging down from the top shelf of the bookcase and he banged the door shut to frighten it away. Now he knocks with his fist on the wall behind him and that puts an end to the scuffling, although he can still imagine the rat in the darkness, crouched on its haunches, pausing in its work. Another sound, a soft whimpering that must be the boy in the room next door, and a bird has just started to sing, perched in the tree that grows outside the window.

He pulls back the tight covering of sheets and blankets and climbs out of bed. He walks to the window which is open so that the cold air creeps around his belly. It has been snowing; the garden is hidden in a cloak of whiteness so that it's like looking out across an ocean with no land anywhere in sight.

He opens the bedroom door as quietly as he can and walks out on to the landing and down the red-carpeted stairs. There is the picture of Jesus as The Light of the World with the lamp that he holds casting sinister shadows across his face, and there is the painting of the sunset over a calm sea which looks dangerous as well, as if something is about to burst out of the smooth blood-red water.

He opens the heavy door to the library, surprised by the coldness of the brass handle as it presses against his palm. Everything is as it was when he last saw it: the leather belt curled up on the shiny mahogany table, the clock twitching within its glass dome, the french windows into the garden reflecting the dazzle of snow outside. He realises with a jolt of surprise that almost nothing here belongs to him, it all comes from his wife's family; it is her furniture, her mohair rug, her brass candlesticks, her domed clock. The belt is his, of course, although it should be back in the bedroom, it looks out of place here. He does own a few books, including the one that Mr Swann gave him, and there is a single photograph that he stuck unobtrusively into one of the family albums: a faded print showing a wooden house built in the colonial style with a forest all around and a high waterfall in the distance. No one has ever noticed it or asked him where it came from and even if they did he might pretend not to know. But there is something else, that statue of the Greek youth plucking a thorn from the sole of his foot; he bought it years ago when he stopped in Paris on his way to England because the figure of the youth reminded him of the mulatto. He stands beside it now and runs his fingers down the naked spine and over the contours of the bronze curls. But he doesn't want to think about the mulatto, and he turns away abruptly from the mantelpiece. He notices a leather-bound book lying under the table; the cover seems to be badly damaged as if it has been chewed; perhaps the rats got it.

He steps out through the french windows and into the garden. The snow is cold under his bare feet, the air snatches at his body, the mist all around him makes him feel disoriented and confused. He walks uncertainly across the lawn, blundering into the flower-beds that are concealed by the snow and knocking his head against the overhanging branch of the cedar tree, until finally he reaches the little gate and enters the grave-yard. He looks for the tombstone that has the same boy's name written on it three times as if the same person had been re-born over and over again, but a pale lichen has covered the stones, obliterating all the names. He remembers the story that Evalina told him about a man who was cursed by a sorcerer and who jumped three times from the high cliffs where the Black River joins the sea and when he was finally dead with the third jump the curse fell on his son so that the boy went mad and no one could stop him or hold him down. Maybe the boy on the tombstone had been cursed by a sorcerer and that was why he kept on dying.

He is inside the church now, the air smelling of damp stone. Just as he has done so often before, he climbs up the little flight of steps that lead to the pul-pit and he stands there in his pyjamas, looking out across the empty pews, the gleam of a brass memorial plaque on the wall, the bright colours of a stained-glass window that shows Paradise as an English landscape with an apple orchard and rolling hills and two swans mirrored by their own reflection in the clear water of a lake. He is filled by a sense of weariness and sadness, a feeling of being far from home, his feet cold, his body cold from the first day that he arrived in this country where he was not born.

'And after that,' he says, his voice echoing through the empty building, 'after that I said this is no place for a man to live. This place is too cold for anyone to live in, I said', and he sings the song that his mother used to sing to him long ago, the one with the chorus that has no meaning,

*Ela le la la*
*Ela le lololo*
*Elale le la e lololo*

Then my grandfather feels very lonely. He leaves the church and returns quickly to the house. He goes into the kitchen and taking a glass bowl he half fills it with a mixture of peroxide and the juice of a lemon, the two liquids fizzing angrily when they are combined.

He walks up the stairs and into the child's bedroom. He kneels beside the bed. He takes a little tin out of his pocket and puts a sprinkling of grey powder on the tip of his tongue. He dips a wad of cotton-wool into the bowl and begins to wash the sleeping face, careful to avoid the eyes.

# Twenty-nine

My grandfather seems to have grown smaller during the night, smaller and more frail as if all his remaining strength has been sucked out of him and even his bones are now as hollow as a bird's. He looks like a sick child, the pillows huge around his head, his little arms limp and exhausted on the sheets, the contours of his body hardly perceptible under the covers.

He gazes at me with a blank expression, the eyes exhausted by old age, but there is a flicker of recognition as he beckons me to come closer, waving his index finger from side to side like the antenna of an insect.

I sit on the edge of the bed and wait. 'Let's go for a walk,' he says in a voice that is so tiny I have to bend forward to catch the words before they evaporate. 'You can put me in a wheelchair and we can go for a walk. We could go anywhere. We could look out of the window. From my bed all that I can see is the sky changing colour, and even when I am in the other room I am always over by the wall on the far side and I can't see anything except that silly man with his dominoes and the television in the distance. But we could look out, couldn't we?'

He smiles shyly and hopefully, panting a little from the effort of so much talk. I am sure that no one would object and anyway there is no one here apart from the bird-reptile man who is still lost in sleep with his eyes sealed tight shut. So I go and fetch a wheelchair from the corridor and position it beside the bed. Very carefully I peel back the covers and expose the tapering body in its striped pyjamas. Very carefully I slip one hand under the insect knees and one hand around the hollow back and with hardly any effort I am lifting my grandfather up in my arms. There is no resistance in him, no tensing of muscles as he leans his weightless head against my shoulder. I used to have a dream in which I had to carry an old man, but in the dream the figure was heavy and threatening, gripping at me like quicksand and pulling me down into obliteration, but this old man has no danger left in him, none at all. I lower him into the wheelchair and he crumples into the seat with a sigh, holding my hand in a gesture of thanks, his hand as soft as a fish.

'Where shall we go first?' I ask him.

By way of reply he inclines his head forward, to

indicate the direction of the nearest window. So we go to the window and it seems like a long journey even though it is no distance at all, only a few paces across the glistening floor. When we arrive I push the side of the chair as close as possible to the window and by turning his head slightly my grandfather can lean his cheek against the glass and look out.

'What do you see?' I ask him.

He is silent for a moment, concentrating. When he does speak his voice is no longer so weak, although it is curiously monotoned as if he is talking in his sleep. 'We are approaching an island,' he says, 'or the island is approaching us, it's hard to tell. There are the birds, there are the trees, there is the sand, there is the sky. There is my cat hunting for a rat. There is the house—what a small house it is and I thought it was much more grand—and the curtains are blowing out of the open windows and my mother is lying on her bed wrapped in a white counterpane. And look, over there where there are more trees and they are thicker and darker, you can just see the other house. I never realised they were so close together, I could have gone from the one to the other if I had known. And that's my pig racing through the trees as if his life depended on it. I used to have a pig as a pet and now there it is. I thought it had been killed during the storm, so that's good.

'Oh but it's changing,' says my grandfather with an edge of panic in his voice. 'The sea has become solid and still and it's not the sea at all, it's the moorland all around me and what I thought were waves are the undulating hills that go on for miles and miles with nothing but the sheep losing each other and the grouse getting frightened and crying "go-back, go-back, go-back". That dark line is Hadrian's Wall, keeping out the enemy from the north, and the little figures are the soldiers who guard it, watching day and night for signs of danger. Did you know that most of them are foreigners with dark skins who came here from places like Morocco and Turkey? They must have been cold with the north wind blowing through them and everything so different from what they had expected.

'You follow the Wall and you come to the sea, but a different coloured sea from the one I was used to. That's me over there, walking along the coast path near the ruin of a big castle that was built to keep the Vikings out. Maybe if we looked long enough we might see the Vikings with bulls' horns on their helmets and the icy blue eyes of my wife's family. You can tell it's me walking because of the way I clasp my hands behind my back, just like your father does. I often spent hours here, up and down along the sand with a jabber of thoughts in my head, and sometimes a seal would push its sweet face through the surface of the sea, as beauti-

ful as a woman with black eyes. The little dunlins flying in gusts just ahead of me and the terns dropping
like gunshot into the water. Sand eels, that's what they
were after; there are no sea slugs or venus girdles here,
no land crabs scuttling like red hands.

'But it's all gone now and I can't see anything
except for a car park and a street and houses in the
rain.'

He turns away from the window and fumbles with
the pocket of his pyjamas. 'I bet you don't know what
I've got here,' he says, and he springs open his hand to
reveal the little tin of powder that Evalina gave him to
protect him from the power of evil.

'Here you are,' he says. 'You can have it. Do what
you like with it. Keep it or throw it away. Don't breathe
it in though, it might make you sneeze. It's very good
for headaches and it will help you to sleep. You just put
a little pinch of it on your tongue, I'll show you', and he
grips the lid of the box with all his strength and tugs at
it. The little tin falls open abruptly, spilling a heap of
dusty powder on his lap.

'Oh well,' he says, brushing the powder to the floor
with a gesture of impatience. 'That's gone then. But I
suppose it might have lost its strength, it is very old. I
had a whole box of things I could have given you, but
the nurse threw them away some time ago. And now
everything has gone, hasn't it?'

He yawns, showing his pink tortoise tongue. 'Will you do something for me, before you go? Will you whisk me around? Round and round, one two three, one two three, whisking round and round. I would like that very much.'

I do what is asked of me and lift him up, scooping him into my arms, as light as a feather, as loose as a string puppet, and with his weightless head leaning once more against my shoulder we spin round and round, faster and faster.

When I lower him back on the bed he looks quite peaceful, his eyes closed and a faint smile on his lips. He takes hold of the sheet in both hands and pulls it up over his head.

'Why are you doing that?' I ask.

'Because I am dead,' he says, and he is so still that I can't even see the movement of his breathing.

Part IV

# Thirty

Ihave become a child again; I know I have
because everything around me is so high, so
hard to reach. I am going down some stairs, one hand
holding the carved railing to steady myself, and each
step I take involves an immense effort of determination
and concentration. I did fall once long ago, the world
suddenly skidding away beneath me as I thudded down
the steps, but that won't happen now because I am
being very careful.

I have reached the foot of the stairs and there is a
door. I can just manage to turn the handle and the
door swings open into a room that is familiar although
I cannot quite remember where I have known it before.
My father is over on the far side of this room, sitting on
a chair, his hands cupped around his head. He is crying,
great lurching sobs that make his whole body shake. I
walk up to him and stand next to him; we are almost
the same height now that he is sitting down.

'What is the matter?' I say. 'What has happened? Can I help you?' but I don't think he can see me or hear me.

A woman in a white uniform comes in and takes his arm, leading him away. He walks like a very old man with slow shuffling steps, his head bent forward to his chest. I watch him go and then I climb into the chair and sit there in silence.

I sit there and see my father as I have known him through the years of my childhood. I see him staring into a mirror until both of us are sure that at any moment he will turn into some terrible wolf-like creature with sharp teeth. He bares his teeth and I hold my breath. I see him walking towards a man and the two of them dance together, wrapped in an embrace, but then he screams as if he has been wounded and grabs the man by the shoulders, pushing him backwards towards an open window. As the man falls from the window a shower of coins erupts in a silver fountain from his trouser pocket.

Now my father is crouched in front of a naked woman on a bed and he is shaking her and shaking her so that her dark hair covers her face and her body is limp. Now he is coming towards me. He seizes the chair in which I am sitting and raises it high above his head before smashing it against a glass door that explodes into a thousand glinting pieces. I am catapulted in a wide arc through the air, but I land safe and unharmed. I go to hide under a table and that's where I find the pig, oblivious of the storms that are raging and preoccupied with the business of chewing at the leather cover of an old book.

But my father is crawling towards me across the floor. He is snarling and snapping like a dog, his eyes red, froth on his lips. Somewhere in the distance a clock is chiming. I lean against the warm tight body of the pig and close my eyes. When I open them again my father has disappeared. I wonder where he has gone. I hope he has stopped crying.

# Thirty-one

The woman in the white uniform led the man away to another part of the building. He was put to bed and he fell asleep almost immediately. In his dream he was standing on a moonlit sea. The water was ruffled by the zig-zag movement of the currents but there were no waves, not even the gentlest undulation. The moonlight glinted and shuddered in the illuminated darkness; it scratched paths of light across the immensity of water. Suddenly he was rushing towards the shore, as if he was a fish on a hook being pulled in, the wheel turning and the thread that held him getting shorter and shorter. He could see a jagged coastline of high cliffs, but then within that same moment everything returned to stillness and he was once more surrounded by a huge rippling sea.

The man wakes up. He is lying in a dark room but it is an unnatural darkness that surrounds him, a darkness made from drawn blinds and screens, from closed doors and bolted windows. Even though it is night all around him he has the sense that somewhere outside it must be day, with pale autumn sunshine and the leaves on the trees turning red.

The man's mouth is dry, his tongue is thick and sluggish. He opens his mouth wide and he can feel the muscles stretching from cheek to jawbone. He has a notebook somewhere—it must be in the black metal trunk that his father gave him so many years ago—and in this notebook he has collected all sorts of pictures that interested him for one reason or another. There is a newspaper photograph of a murderer looking very quiet and wistful, a voodoo dancer with a snake creeping into his mouth, a hippopotamus in a wallow of mud, a boxer's face contorted with the impact of a blow. There is a portrait of Caitlin Thomas, the poet's wife, her body as solid as a seal, and he remembers trying to kiss her at a party and how dense her flesh felt under his hands. But it is the painting of the working of the muscles and tendons that he is thinking of now; an Italian painting, eighteenth century or thereabouts. A man leans against a wall, his chin resting thoughtfully on his hand, one elegant leg bent at the knee, and all his skin has been pulled away to reveal the red curtains of muscles and tendons that make movement possible, whether for a fleeting smile or a sudden lurching step forward. A flayed man, and in Mexico and in the

Middle Ages they did used to strip the living form like that. He wonders if the body beneath the skin can stay alive, at least for a little while. Probably not. And can the Ethiopian change his skin, remove one and put on another like a new suit of clothes? That was the theme of his father's favourite sermon and he can see him now, standing in the damp grey church, holding on to the pulpit as if he was at the prow of a ship with the waves crashing around him. His voice is solemn but strident to the edge of hysteria, echoing around that gloomy building and settling on the heads of the congregation. No, the Ethiopian cannot change his skin, that was the gist of the argument. Blackness cannot be turned into whiteness. The sinner cannot escape from his sin.

The man in the dark room taps his teeth with his fingernail. Big solid horse-like teeth and presumably you can tell a person's age from the teeth just as well; lifting the slave's lips before discussing a price. Curiously personal things teeth are. He found a skull once on the beach when he was walking there as a child near a ruined castle that grew like an old tree among the smooth boulders, and the skull must have come from a graveyard somewhere nearby. The cavity was packed full of earth and there were threads of roots growing in it, but it was the teeth that impressed him, they were so intimate. He bites at the tip of his finger, testing the threshold of pain.

The isolation here is extraordinary. Sometimes he holds his left hand in his right hand for comfort when he feels in danger of losing all sense of inhabiting a body. Time congeals around him without definition. In theory he is supposed to be asleep, that was the idea, a dense descent into a sleep so deep that it would shake off the darkness that was lodged inside him, the despair. The doctor who explained the process was very confident. 'Oh yes,' he had said from behind his big desk, rubbing his fat hands together like Pontius Pilate. 'Oh yes, we have a very successful programme; our patients wake up renewed, resurrected you might say, all trouble forgotten.'

But instead he was here in this darkness, all troubles remembered, filled with whatever drugs were supposed to drift him into an empty sleep, and he was not asleep at all, or at least only fitfully and when he did sleep his mind raced with endless dreams.

He had sat with the doctor in the consulting-room, his head sagging between his shoulders, and the doctor had said, 'How do you feel?' staring at him with round fish eyes, the blue irises swimming in little pools of clear water. 'How do you feel? Can you try to tell me?'

'Soot,' he had replied. 'My mouth is filled with soot, my body is filled with soot, acrid and bitter, clogging the arteries and the pores. I am like Blake's chimney-sweep who could only say "peep, peep, peep".

And blood, I can taste blood as well, salty and not at all nice.' He had smiled an odd lop-sided smile and the doctor had smiled back at him. They were conspirators tangled in the same plot.

And so they admitted him to hospital for treatment. He was washed and brushed and dressed in new striped pyjamas and told that everything would be fine. He caught a glimpse of himself in a long mirror in the bathroom and that gave him quite a shock. He looked just like his own father, the same quivering lip, tortoise tongue, wolfish stare, wavering steps. It was as if the old man had jumped on to his back and enveloped him.

They gave him an injection and then he was on a trolley-bed being wheeled along endless corridors with the strips of light whizzing above his head like shooting stars. And then the lights were out and he was here, waiting.

He sniffs the air. Can he smell camphor or is it only his imagination? As a child he was always terrified of the dark. Once when it was cold his mother covered him with a fur rug while he was sleeping and when he woke he thought he had turned into an animal, a great shaggy beast that could shake off its disguise when the moon was full. Shake it off or peel it back. He had read somewhere that the werewolf's fur was on the under-side of its human skin so that all it needed to do was to turn itself inside out.

He rubs his face with his hand, gently around the eye sockets, along the ridge of the nose, down the cheeks that are rough and unshaven. He remembers how his face used to sting after his father had washed it with peroxide, and sometimes he felt as if the outer surface would peel away like the skin of an orange. He remembers the smell that hooked into his nostrils and at the back of his throat. He remembers everything as if it were still happening now, as if it had never ceased to happen.

# Thirty-two

The man was dreaming of foxes. He was staring up at a forest that stood right on the edge of a steep bank of earth, and as he grew accustomed to the shaded darkness between the trees he began to see the red shapes of foxes. There were hundreds of them, a tangled crowd of life flickering like flames.

When he slides back into wakefulness the man continues to search the darkness for the glint of foxes, but slowly he realises that they have gone and he has lost them. He had two fox cubs once, long ago. He found them washed up on the river bank after a storm and he kept them secretly in a shepherd's hut on the edge of the moor. He fed them on rats, rabbits, birds, anything he could find. He had forgotten all about them but the dream brought them back.

The dream brought them back. How he would creep out of the house very early in the morning; through his bedroom window, down the ivy, across the wet grass with a grey misty light spreading around him and the first birds singing. Through the little gate and into the churchyard where the heavy gravestones were tipped and tilted this way and that as if the dead were pushing through the weight of the earth. And then it was only a short distance to the moor and the little hut.

He always knocked on the door of the hut before entering and the fox cubs would welcome him with a rush of yammering snickering cries that he can hear even now when he listens carefully. As soon as he was inside they would clamber up his trouser leg and on to his shoulders, grasping at him with cat-like claws. Then he would produce his offering of food and sit and watch them while they ate, snapping and growling at each other in mock ferocity as all that fur and bone disappeared into their swollen bellies. Once they had been fed they didn't mind being stroked, although they never kept still for long and never closed their mad yellow eyes, not for a second. He loved the sharp stink of them. His first wife had smelt like that sometimes, as sharp as a fox and her hair was red. Strange to think of her as being dead, earth hammering on the lid of her coffin and the rain as well.

One morning he approached the hut and heard the cubs screeching as if they were in pain. He heard their claws scrabbling desperately at the glass of the window as if they were trying to escape from an enemy. He burst in thinking that he had come just in time to save them but there was nothing there to harm them, nothing had changed except that they wanted their freedom.

He kept them for only a few more days after that. They no longer welcomed him when he visited them and they had no interest in food. The ratcatcher who lived in the village told him that a fox will bite through its own leg in order to rid itself of the wire noose that holds it and he realised that his foxes would die if he didn't release them. So he opened the door and they darted out and raced across the moor without a backward glance, leaving him with only the trace of their peppery smell. After they had gone he still went regularly to the hut for several months, hoping that they might return and hover close to him if only for a few moments. Since no one had any use for the hut he made it into a sort of museum which he filled with a collection of treasures: a white seagull feather, a few eggs, stones with a pattern that attracted him and a little piece of red coral that he found in a flower-bed close to the rose bush. He often wondered where it had come from.

He puts the memory of that piece of coral into the palm of his hand and strokes it gently. He is the fox now. The fox locked in a hut, caught in a trap. It is not just the dark room that holds him, it is the despair that grips into his skull like a wire noose, tighter and tighter until he will have to bite off his own head to get free from it.

He had done his best to escape. He had tried drinking until he could no longer stand but lay thrashing on the floor, and he had combined that with all sorts of pills mixed and crunched together. There was one new type of pill that was supposed to incapacitate wild animals that needed to be moved from one place to another, but they only made him feel like a rhinoceros, with a heavy awkward body and danger on all sides. No quiet there, just the beat of drums, the sound of gunshot.

A previous doctor had suggested electric shock treatment. 'I believe it will help to simplify matters,' he said, pressing the tips of his fingers together as if to connect the circuit and start the procedure straight-away. This doctor wore a black bow-tie and his lips were so surprisingly red that the man was glad to agree to anything he suggested just so as to bring their conversation to an end. He remembers how he queued up with the others, waiting patiently for his turn on the machine, excited by the ritual of being prepared for execution, the solemnity of the occasion. He was looking forward to the moment when that flood of electricity would reduce everything in his mind to a heap of mud and rubble.

But it didn't make him forget, not at all. It was as if

one shock reminded him of other shocks and he was made to hurtle back and back until he had entered a past that was not his at all. There was the image of a woman he had never seen before, lifting a white night-dress up over her head, her dark body hanging like a fruit, her feet so cold and reptilian. There was a naked man on all fours with the face of a pig; a dead monkey with a fruit trapped in its mouth giving it a look of extreme surprise; pale trees that had the bodies of naked people; and thick black slug-like creatures shuffling in a silent army across the sand of a beach. And there was also the image of someone who seemed to be himself but changed beyond all recognition, snapping and snarling like a mad beast. Only occasionally was the horror of these unremembered memories lifted and that was when he caught a glimpse of a child who seemed to be watching him from a safe distance; staring at him with dark unquestioning eyes that were somehow familiar.

There is a bell beside the bed. He leans over and presses it until he thinks he can hear the sound it is making, jangling somewhere in the upper storeys of this building. In a little while someone will come. Someone will switch on the dim red light and ask him what is the matter, does he need something. 'I can't sleep,' he will say. 'Please help me, I can't sleep.'

# Thirty-three

It can't have been long after the dream of foxes that the man escaped. He had been brought up out of the darkness and given a bed in a narrow room with a wall on one side of him and a young man with a face like the moon on the other. The young man used to weep softly all through the night because he wanted to be turned into a woman and no one would help him.

The man behaved well. He did what he was told. Every morning he swallowed his pills with water from a tiny plastic cup. He wore slippers and watched horse-racing on television. At around midday he was expected to join a discussion group where patients talked about their problems. In the afternoon he was often asked to show people the way to the ECT room and he sometimes waited with them in the queue, telling them not to worry, they would come to no harm. There was a woman who had lost her right arm when she threw herself on to a railway line and he was happy to sit beside her during mealtimes, cutting up the food on her plate and steering the fork towards her mouth. He offered to help with the game of Bingo that was held every Monday and Wednesday. He would look at everyone's cards to see if there was a number that was the same as the number being called out, and if he found one he shouted 'Bingo!' so loud that he created a startled silence all around him.

And then he escaped. It was quite easy. He found a pair of shoes, a jacket and some trousers in a cupboard and he put them on. The trousers were quite a good fit and so were the shoes, although he had no socks and wondered if anyone would notice. The jacket was far too tight, he could hardly move his arms and the buttons wouldn't do up, but that didn't matter and the pyjama top could masquerade as a shirt. He wondered where his own clothes had been put, he would have liked to see his white linen suit again because he was very fond of it.

No one bothered to ask him where he was going when he walked out of the room, looking neither to the left or the right, his feet clicking nervously on the shiny floor. Along a corridor, down some stairs and then it was simply a question of following the signs that said Exit. He paused by the flower-stall and would have liked to buy himself a bunch of roses but he had

no money. Then he approached the big automatic
doors and they slid open obediently as soon as they felt
the weight of his body.

He was out in the world. He trod in a puddle and
the cold water crept into his shoes. He was startled by
all the noise and activity and for several minutes he
stood quite still while people pushed past him and
bright metal cars roared along the road like shoals
of fish.

He decided to go to the park because that seemed
like a good idea and he knew it was not far away. He
found it eventually and the moment he stepped
through the high metal gates he felt much quieter in
himself. There in front of him was the familiar path
that led up the hill and round towards the wood.

He was trotting now, his arms bent slightly at the
elbow in spite of the constriction of the jacket and his
heart thumping at the back of his throat. Here were
the rhododendron bushes and beyond them the beech
trees that he had watched through so many seasons.
He ducked his head to avoid an overhanging branch,
but failed to notice a root that stretched long fingers
across the path and so he tripped and fell. He fell
slowly, like a bird falling out of the sky with its wings
still catching the lift of the air as it spirals down. He
could see himself toppling towards the ground and
when he landed he seemed to bounce and roll over

with infinite lassitude until finally he was lying on his back, huge and helpless. He looked up at the tracery of leaves above him and some of them were fluttering in the air like red butterflies.

A woman and a dog were coming along the path towards him. The dog was a stiff-legged Jack Russell terrier, rather similar to the one that he had kept for many years, and when it reached him it paused, sniffed at his body and seemed to be about to cock its leg against him but the woman called out sharp and urgent and it turned and pattered away obediently, the tail erect. Then the woman might have come up to him to ask if he was all right. She might have knelt beside him, her face close and anxious, asking if he was hurt in any way. He would have replied, 'Thank you, I'm quite all right', smiling to show that he meant it. But the woman had gone.

With difficulty he got back on his feet. There was mud on his trousers now and on his jacket as well, but he could brush it off later when it had dried. He was hungry and wished he had something to eat, but that could also come later, there was no hurry.

He was heading towards a tree that he knew well, a huge oak which had been blasted by lightning that had struck off its upper branches, leaving it with a blackened hollow stump and two surviving branches stretching out one on either side of the trunk like open arms. He had always been fond of this tree and when he reached it now he felt as if he was meeting with an old friend whom he had despaired of ever seeing again.

He stroked the rough bark. He wanted to raise his arms high above his head but the jacket held him back and he could feel it tensing and splitting along the seams, so he took it off and placed it neatly folded on the ground. He took his shoes off as well because he knew that the soles were so slippery and he put them side by side next to the jacket.

Now he was ready. He reached up and grasped hold of one of the branches. He was shocked to see his own hands, so big and swollen and red-fingered like crabs. When had he become so heavy? He used to have a thin body that was easy to stretch and move, but instead he had become enveloped by this strange unwieldy bulki-ness, he was trapped inside it like a tortoise in its shell.

With an immense effort he managed to heave him-self up into the tree and over a branch until he could lie along it, his heart pounding in his forehead, his skin soaked with sweat. But at least he had done what he meant to do and it was only a few careful steps further to the broken centre of the tree where he knew there was a hollow space just wide enough to sit in, comfort-able and protected, safe from harm. He used to come here quite often simply because it was a pleasant place to be, with the leaves all around him, the soft smells, the sense of being suspended just above the world. Sometimes people would walk past or even sit on the ground beneath him, their backs leaning against the trunk, and he could listen to their talk and their movements. Once a child had climbed up and found him in his nest, but didn't seem at all surprised, just stared at him with dark unquestioning eyes and then went away silently.

He sits there unseen. A thin drizzle is soaking into his hair and skin. There is a tiny scattering of movement just above his head and he looks up to see a wren searching for insects in the thick crevices of the bark. It's so close that he could almost reach out his hand and touch the delicate body with the tips of his fingers. It starts to sing and the sound is so wild and strident that it makes him cry, the tears wet on his face that is already wet from the rain.

# Thirty-four

So that's it. All done and over with. The house has been walked through. I have entered as many rooms as I could find and I have tried to describe what I saw there. I have come back outside now and I have just heard the door click shut behind me. The pig is walking off into the distance, unconcerned.

# About the Author

Julia Blackburn lives in Suffolk, England, with her husband and two children. She is the daughter of the English poet Thomas Blackburn (1916–1977), whose family originally came from Mauritius. She is the author of *The Emperor's Last Island* and *Daisy Bates in the Desert*.